three
love by numbers #3

e.s. carter

*Justine
"Acceptance is serenity"
ES Carter*

Copyright 2015 by E.S. Carter
All rights reserved.
Cover Design by Cover Me Darling
Cover image licensed from Fotolia.
Formatted by Marisa-rose Shor of Cover Me, Darling and
Allyson Gottlieb of Athena Interior Book Design

This book, or parts thereof, may not be reproduced in any form without expressed written permission from the author; exceptions are made for brief excerpts used in published reviews.

All trademarks contained in this book, are the property of the respective copyright holders and have been used without permission.

Tell me the story of how the sun loved the moon so much, he died every night to let her breathe.
　　　　　　　　　　　　—Author Unknown.

*To G for being my soul mate and best friend; trust I seek and
I find in you.
To L, G & A for inspiring me to be better.
To P for being the best big brother a girl could ever want.
I miss you.*

three
love by numbers #3

prologue

Liam

Four years ago…

Three.

A cardinal number, a prime number and the sum of two plus one.

Three strikes and you're out.

Two's company, three's a crowd.

Third time lucky.

These are the random and crazy thoughts that run through my mind as I stand outside room three of the new Art College block.

This may be due to my raging hangover from the excess alcohol I consumed last night, or it may be my brain's way of dealing with the teenage nerves flying through my system; nerves that stem from finally following my dreams in spite of my parents' doubts.

Whatever the reason, standing in that narrow

hallway, staring at a bland white door with a small grid window at the top and a basic, black metal three screwed below, allows their doubts to fester within me.

No.

I shake my head to get rid of the abstract thoughts that are fuelled by my childish fears and run a hand through my unruly hair.

I'm doing this.

I'm proving to them that I can make my love for art become more than just a hobby and if I have to take night classes in a community college, alongside my school studies, then so be it.

Three; the number of steps I take into the room before I see her.

The early evening sun sits low on the horizon and bathes the classroom with a hazy glow, causing her sleek, auburn hair to shine like burnished gold.

She's petite, probably a little over five foot and the tips of her hair rest just above the waist of her dark, skinny jeans. Following the tight, dark denim down over areas I should not be staring at, my eyes come to rest on the well-worn, red Converse on her feet. She absentmindedly crosses one foot over the other; standing in a pose that looks uncomfortable, yet on her seems natural.

Dragging my eyes back up over her form, I only get to see her profile briefly as she bends over another student's desk, placing a blank piece of paper in front of him, before she moves on to the next table.

She's pale, with a smattering of light freckles across her nose and cheeks and she has the longest eyelashes I have ever seen. It's only when she turns to face me that I get hit with the full force of her striking, emerald green eyes; eyes that are currently looking past me, towards another tardy student entering the room.

"Take a seat, gentlemen, please."

Her raspy voice does not fit her petite stature; it's husky, low and vibrates deep in my gut.

The student behind me pushes past my immobile body and into the seat directly in front of me, all the while I stand frozen, unable to tell my limbs to function. My teenage brain is completely fried by the voice of the woman standing before me.

Not just any woman, the voice of the teacher, my teacher, standing before me.

"Last seat is yours or have you come to the wrong class? Photography is just down the hall in room five or still life classes are next door in room four."

She smiles at me and my traitorous body tightens all over.

My imbecilic mind tells my useless mouth to mirror her smile.

Confusion crosses her idyllic features and her brow furrows at the obviously moronic look on my face. Yet I still cannot form words.

Talking slowly, she approaches me, "Hey, do you

need some help? Are you in the right place?"

Her tone is soft, sensitive and careful, but the throaty quality of her voice remains. It rushes through my blood, creeping into parts of my body that would be highly inappropriate to have stimulated right now.

I force my brain to work, pushing my croaky words over my thick tongue and out into the space between us.

"I'm here for the art class."

Doh.

Of course, I'm here for the art class. State the obvious idiot.

She grants me a slight smile before turning towards the front of the class and motioning with her hand to the only free seat available, smack bang in the first row.

Normally I would avoid the front row like the plague. No typical boy my age would willingly choose to sit there, much preferring the comfort and anonymity of the back row, but I find myself uncharacteristically happy to be that much closer to her.

"Students, I am Miss Pritchard and this is your first art class of the year."

She looks out at her room full of students, eyes skimming over all the faces, never lingering on anyone but greeting everyone with a warm smile.

"Today is about me getting to know you better and by that I don't just mean your names or your preferred medium. I want to get to know you from the inside out."

She lets her words register on her rapt audience and I am sure every person in this room is as captivated with her as I am.

"In front of you is a blank piece of paper. Use whatever supplies you have brought with you, be it a pen, pencil, charcoal, pastels, anything you have to hand and draw me your heart."

A few murmurs of questions hit the air and she gracefully reaches her hand up to silence them.

"I don't mean literally draw me your heart, I want you to dig deep and draw me what's inside of your heart. What makes you, what drives you, what inspires you, what makes you feel? This is open to interpretation and there are no wrong choices. How can what you feel inside, what is part of your heart, ever be wrong?"

Three…is a magic number.

I tear my eyes from the mesmerizing and completely unobtainable woman in front of me, grab my rucksack off the floor, dig out my charcoals and proceed to draw her my heart.

My foolish, infatuated, teenage heart.

The rule of three.

Three blind mice.

Three sides to a triangle.

Three; the number of times I restart my piece before I am happy with the shape of her eyes and the formation of freckles across the bridge of her nose.

chapter 1

Liam

"Jules, don't panic. I'll be back in plenty of time for your big day. Do you really think I'd miss out on watching you ball and chain Jake?"

I survey the security camera screens in front of me while listening to her reply.

"Liam, can you be serious for just one second? I miss you, *we miss you*. I'm just making sure you know how important it is to us to have you home this weekend. It's been months since we saw you last and that's only because we visited you. The club can manage without you for the next week I'm sure."

I run a hand over my face and exhale loudly.

"Seriously Jules, I'll be there. No need to panic, or are you turning into one of those crazy bridezillas? Tut tut Jules, I thought you had more class."

I don't even attempt to hide the smile from my voice. It's always been easy to rile her up and she never takes my banter to heart. She's like the sister I

three

never had and I am genuinely over the moon that she is marrying my brother. If anyone was going to tame Jake's wild ways, I knew it would be Jules.

"I swear I will bridezilla your arse if you're not back in time Liam. Do you have your flight booked or do you need me to arrange it? I know how useless you are and I'm not giving you any excuse to bail on us."

As the last word passes her lips, a commotion on one of the screens before me catches my eye.

"I've got it covered Jules, stop stressing. Now I have to go, some idiot is causing a scene in Aurora. Say Hi to everyone for me and I'll see you soon."

I stand, grab my keys from the desk in front of me and leave my office quickly, locking the door securely behind me.

"Love you Li, see you this weekend."

Pocketing my keys, I stride towards the concealed doors that lead out into the main club.

"Love you Jules. If you're really lucky I won't embarrass you during the speeches by telling everyone how you got your nickname."

I hear her gasp as she tries to muffle her laughter, but I cut her off before she can speak further.

"I really do have to go; I'll call you when I get my flight details. Miss you."

I hang up, not waiting for her response. Jules really can talk for hours on the phone if you let her and with a packed club, in the middle of the main tourist season, I have work to do.

It's funny to think that I am now doing the job that was once hers. When Jules—or Emma to everyone else—decided to take Jake up on his offer to travel the world during his promotional tour for the huge TV series, *Vampires Bite*, no-one was more surprised than I.

Yes, you guessed it. The *Jake Fox* aka bad boy vampire, *Cole Creed* is my brother. I'm the baby of the family and totally overshadowed by each of my older brothers.

Jake is by far the most famous, but each of them are successful in their own right, while I just work for one of them.

Nate, my eldest brother, owns a successful group of nightclubs that span across Europe and I run his Ibiza venue, Accede.

It's a cool gig, I get to spend the evenings in a vibrant atmosphere, surrounded by Europe's most beautiful people and I laze my days away on some of the most idyllic beaches in the world.

Yeah, it's tough being me.

I should be living the life, partying hard, having a different woman in my bed every night.

I should be, but I'm not.

It's not my style.

I might envy my two eldest brother's success but I do not emulate their former *manwhore* lifestyles. Besides, both have settled down now. Jake is about to marry Emma and Nate is still going strong with Liv and that is what I envy the most; I envy the fact that they get to keep the *one*.

That one person you know was put on this earth just for you.

Your missing piece.

I force my thoughts to stop.

I don't want to walk down memory lane right now.

I don't want to remember the pain in my chest when she crushed my heart.

I'm weak, I admit that.

I'm almost twenty-three years old and I refuse to move on from the only woman I've ever been with. The only woman I ever gave myself to.

The trouble is when I gave myself to her, I gave her my entire being.

My heart, my soul, my blood, my bones.

It wasn't enough.

I wasn't enough.

She chose someone else, someone who already filled her heart and I despise the person who gets to have her love. I despise them with all the parts of me that I freely gave to her.

My heart, my soul, my blood, my bones.

I curse under my breath and step out onto the terrace of Aurora.

Since Nate opened this place around eighteen months ago, it's been a huge success. Tonight is no different. Even though it's close to 3 am, the place is still buzzing.

Scanning the crowd of clubbers before me, I spot security escorting the guy who was causing the trouble moments earlier, from the premises.

One less thing for me to deal with.

I'm about to turn and do a check on the bar staff and kitchen, when my eyes catch on a girl sitting alone on one of the large, sectional outdoor sofas. Her tear stained face is fixed on the two security guards who are leading the troublemaker from the club.

Her makeup is smeared, her vibrant auburn hair is escaping from the clip she has used to pin it back, framing her in fiery, disheveled strands.

I don't know if it's her hair colouring, reminding me of someone I fight every day to forget, or if it's the look of utter desolation on her face but my feet are already dragging my body towards her, before my mind has even caught up.

I stand just to the side of her, close enough that she is aware of my presence but far enough away so that I'm not encroaching her personal space.

Up close she looks young, old enough to be clubbing but too young to look as devastated as she

three

does.

Her chocolate brown eyes are rimmed with smudged eyeliner, tears still freely flowing down her cheeks.

"Hey, are you okay? Can I help in any way?"

My words are soft, low and said in a tone not meant to startle.

Nothing. She doesn't even blink. Her eyes are still transfixed on the exit doors.

I move slowly in front of her and bend to sit on the sofa, my body is at least a foot away from hers but my legs are angled towards her small frame.

"I'm a good listener if you want to talk. I'm sure between us we can fix whatever is making you so sad."

Still nothing. No movement, no acknowledgement, not even a visible intake of breath.

I sigh and look away to the spot that she hasn't yet taken her eyes off. Moments pass between us in silence and I should probably walk away and send one of the female staff members over to see if they can help.

When sun, sea, sex and lots of alcohol get mixed together, you often have this situation, especially at our club because it's open all night.

Tourists enjoying their Ibiza break, over indulge, burn the candle at both ends and then either lose their cool, like the guy I'm guessing has just been kicked out did, or in the case of girls like Miss Auburn, the tears flow.

Alcohol always has a knack of making even the most minor upsets seem like world changing events.

I look over at her once more before rising to leave, Kayleigh or Zoey, two of my staff currently working the bar, can come over and see if Miss Auburn needs help. I'll run the bar while they stem her tears and pack her into a taxi.

I go to step past her and feel a hand grab onto the fabric of my trouser leg, halting me.

Her small, delicate fingers, their nails painted in rainbow colours, grip tightly, creasing the cotton and causing my pant leg to rise.

Looking down at her hand, I turn my head to catch her eye and those chocolate pools, overflowing with salty pain, plead with me to help her.

"I have nowhere to go."

Five words laced with such sadness.

Sadness I am all too familiar with.

Sadness that I hide behind my laid-back veneer.

Sadness that is now rearing its head and recognizing itself in another.

Like they all say, sadness loves company. Or is that misery?

No matter, I know that it's the least I can do to help someone whose face currently reflects the state of my soul.

"We are all lost…until someone finds us."

My softly spoken words gain no response, but I see understanding in her eyes.

I reach my hand out for her to take, "I'd like to

wear these trousers again, in fact, they are currently my favourite pair. If you can take my hand and spare my trousers, I'd be grateful enough to take you to someone who can help you figure something out."

She looks at her hand still clutching the fabric tightly and immediately lets it go. Her eyes flick to my outstretched hand and she hesitates.

"Maybe I should introduce myself, I'm Liam, I run Accede and Aurora and I know that two of my bar staff have a spare room at their place. I'm sure you can crash there, get some sleep and everything will seem clearer."

She glances at my hand again, before placing her palm onto mine.

"Halle."

I stare back at her face, not quite catching her whispered response.

"My name is Halle."

I nod softly, guiding her towards the back of the bar.

"Just like my favourite Bond girl." The words leave my mouth absentmindedly.

We reach the bar and before I leave her to get one of the girls, she clears her throat, her voice coming out louder than before.

"Film buff?"

I turn to face her, noticing that at least her tears have stopped.

"Sorry?" I ask confused.

Her lips quirk in a slight smile.

"You mentioned Bond, I wondered if you were a film buff?"

At this, I give her a genuinely wide smile.

"Jinx, you have no idea."

Her eyebrows lift and her slight smile brightens.

"Jinx?"

I laugh, shaking my head that someone named Halle doesn't know the super sexy, Bond girl alias of her namesake.

"Let me get you a place sorted for tonight and I can educate you in all things Bond tomorrow."

The smile remains as she gives me a soft nod of agreement.

I walk towards a curious looking Kayleigh who has been eyeing our exchange, ready to brief her on the extra roommate she's going to get for tonight.

Just call me Bond.

Liam Bond.

Saviour of teary redheads everywhere.

Except one.

chapter 2

Liam

After handing over Aurora to Rhian, the dayshift manager, I spend a few hours catching up on some sleep at my apartment.

The same apartment that was once Emma's.

Halle stayed with Kayleigh and Zoey until they finished work and they promised to take her home with them until she could sort herself out.

I didn't find out her story or what happened last night. Truth be told, I didn't ask. My knight in shining armour duties only go so far.

In fact, I still don't understand why I wanted to help as much as I did last night. I've seen plenty of tearful girls in the club over the last few months and I've never felt the need to go above and beyond before. It had to be the hair.

Yes, I was a glutton for punishment.

I grab a quick breakfast, breakfast meaning a late lunch for everyone else and then head to the marina to spend a few hours with Marcos on his boat.

I met Marcos during the search for Jake.

My, semi-famous at the time, older brother, got stranded with Emma at a secluded cove and decided to swim for help at night. Yes, at night.

What possessed him to be so bloody stupid, I'll never know, but the days when he was missing, feared dead, almost tore our family apart.

Marcos is a local boat owner who gave his services freely in the search for Jake and now that I am a permanent resident on the island, I spend a lot of time helping him out on his small but perfectly formed, fishing boat.

Around ten years older than me, Marcos returned to the island after he lost his wife and young son in a car accident while living in mainland Spain. He said his heart told him to return to his birthplace. So that's what he did. He'd been back on the island for almost five years and we'd been friends for almost two.

What I liked about Marcos was his ability to still live, not survive.

He talked with joy about his wife and child. The evidence of this love all over his boat, from its name 'Marisa', to the pictures of them all pinned up in the small galley.

He had no desire to date again, saying that his love for Marisa would be unfair to any other woman as it was still as strong as the day he married her, if not more. Yet, he didn't dwell in grief. He celebrated

three

their lives while still living his and even if his life did often seem lonely to me, it worked for him.

"Hey Li, you're just in time to come fishing with me for a few hours. Get up here and sort out the bait and nets, while I get her ready."

Her. He always called his boat 'her', like it was a living being. I guess to him it really was. 'Marisa' gave him much needed solace now that her namesake only lived on in his memories.

"Put me straight to work, no 'Nice to see you Liam', or 'Hey how was your week Liam?'. Good to see my friendship is valued, Cabron."

This earned me a hearty laugh and a clasp of his hand as he hauled me aboard, patting me on the shoulder with a little too much force.

"I'll give you *Cabron,* you little shit. Now, less talk more action. The waves are calling to me and you are eating into my fishing time. You want me to ask about your wellbeing like a best girlfriend? Wait until we are out on open water, I have a reputation of manliness to protect."

He claps me across the face like I'm a good boy and turns on his heels to get the boat ready to cast off. Whistling the whole time while I mutter curses under my breath.

Around forty minutes later we are out on the open sea.

The azure waters are calm, the sun's rays reflect across them making them sparkle, like millions of tiny diamonds floating across the horizon.

I wonder if I could gather them up would I be a rich man?

Not rich in monetary value, rich in serenity, rich in heart.

Would I then resemble these untroubled, glittering waters?

I look over at Marcos, busy with nets and rods. His eyes reflect the shimmer of the ocean, yet also absorb it.

If a man who has lost so much, lost his entire world, can still be worth more than I, can still be rich according to what he is, not what he has, then there is still hope for me.

Still a chance for the storm inside me to transform into halcyon weather.

Still a chance for the ache in my chest, the pathetic unrequited love that marks me, to dissipate. I pray that my heart's inertness ends. I yearn for each beat to fill my body with life.

"Wake up Sunshine, staring at me while daydreaming does not catch fish."

Marcos is setting the rods in their stands, his head is turned in my direction and wrinkles form across his brow as he studies me.

"One so young should not carry the hurt you do. It's time to let it go, Liam. Time to man-up and live life, rather than letting life live you."

three

I blink slowly at his words, the sun reflecting off the water behind him, bathing his form in a halo of light.

The urge to sketch him hits me hard, quickly followed by the shock this realisation has on me.

I haven't wanted to sketch since I left home.

Since I tossed all my art supplies and all my completed works in the trash; since *she* tossed my immature, infatuated heart in the trash.

"Hey Cabron, you look like you've seen a ghost, shake it off my man. No ghosts out here on the water."

His large hand squeezes my shoulder, releasing me from my thoughts.

"Sorry, long night at the club, plus we had some trouble and I had to send a girl home with some of my staff. I guess I needed more sleep."

I offer a lame smile, forcing my eyes to meet his.

Sometimes it's hard to look Marcos in the eye; he misses nothing and sees everything, even the things you bury behind cracks that you've reinforced with cement.

"Okay Cabron, let's fish. You're still losing from last week," he winks before turning back towards his work "on both fish and jokes. I need some new material for those old dogs at the marina."

This is what we do, fish and trade jokes. It's a game to see how many times we can make the other person laugh and I don't mean a polite 'that was funny' laugh, I mean a full belly laugh.

Last week I was all out of jokes, the worry of returning home for Jake and Emma's wedding stealing all the funny right out of my bones.

Not because I don't want to be part of their big day, just because I didn't want to go home and bump into the very person I ran away from in the first place.

"Okay, there are thirty cows in a field, twenty-eight chickens. How many didn't?"

He stills, contemplating my random words.

"That makes no sense, Cabron. I said jokes not riddles."

I repeat my question with a smile in my voice. I know when I've repeated it for the third time that it's starting to piss him off. I know because it pissed my brother Isaac off too when I asked him the same thing.

"How many didn't what?" he growls over his shoulder at me while I chuckle and continue winding the reel on one of my rods.

"There are…" I don't get to repeat the whole question before he angrily butts in.

"I heard you the first time, I don't know how many didn't do whatever-the-fuck they didn't do. This isn't a funny fucking joke!"

I can't help it then, the laugh bubbles up out of my belly and I struggle to form the words.

"There are thirty…"

"Do not fucking repeat it or I'll toss you overboard."

three

"Wait, just wait." I toss my hand up to signal that I just need a minute to compose myself. Once I can speak past my chuckles, I motion to my ear, "Just listen carefully, you grumpy git."

He glares at me and I struggle to not burst into further fits of laughter.

I clear my throat. "There are *thirty* cows in a field, twenty *ate*," I mime biting into an invisible chicken leg, "chickens. How many didn't?"

He looks at me still perplexed before I see clarity wash over his face. He bends down, picking up the box of fish guts we use as bait and in one swift movement dumps it over my head.

"Now that, Cabron, is fucking funny!"

I am dumbstruck for a moment, fish innards running down my face and pooling in the collar of my polo shirt.

When the first roar of laughter leaves my lips, he throws his head back and laughs like an absolute fool.

"You still haven't answered. Makes me wonder if you really did figure out the answer."

He stops laughing and picks up a second box of bait, "Maybe you need a few more, let's say *ten* fish gut showers. Of course I know the fucking answer and *that* is not a joke, so you lose again this week."

I go to protest, a huge grin on my face as he begins to lift the bait box higher.

"Okay, you win. If you need to cheat to beat me, I'm cool with that."

He smiles softly at me the humour of the

moment leaving his face to be replaced with an unknown emotion.

"No, Cabron, you win. That's life I finally see in your eyes and it looks good on you."

Then he turns back around and continues with his tasks, while I stand in the baking hot sun, a small smile on my face, stinking of rotten fish; yet my heart feels freer than it has done in ages.

All thanks to thirty cows that have a taste for poultry.

chapter 3

Liam

Marcos caught more fish than me too and declares that a double victory again this week.

As I walk away from the marina a few hours later, the smell of dead fish burning my nostrils and the remnants of fish guts still sticking to parts of my neck, I hear him talking to a few of the other fishermen and boat owners, "There are thirty cows in a field…" he looks over at me and winks before turning back to his enraptured audience and I can't help but walk back to my apartment feeling lighter, a smile never leaving my lips.

Later that evening, after scrubbing the fish smell from my skin and grabbing a quick tapas meal from a local restaurant, I head to the club for the evening even though it's my night off.

Isaac is meeting me there to take more shots of the club for the glossy magazine he's currently doing an article for.

He's been on the island almost two weeks while he documents the famous nightlife, the beautiful beaches and the even more beautiful partygoers.

Just like all my other brothers, except for Josh, who has never had eyes for anyone other than his wife Laura, Isaac enjoys beauty.

He enjoys a new form of beauty almost every, single, night. Only Isaac finds beauty in both sexes and, at a guess, I'd say he finds it in both sexes at once.

Yes, my brother likes to have his cake and eat it. What's more, he has never hidden this fact. Something I admire him for, although I'd never tell him.

"Hey, Li-Li, sorry to call you in on your night off, although I'm betting you didn't have any other plans."

Isaac smirks at me as I enter my office; he's dressed in typical Isaac fashion of an artsy, grungy look, with a scarf and his camera hanging around his neck.

"I'm almost twenty-three Iz, enough with the Li-Li, we aren't kids anymore."

"You'll always be Li-Li to me, it's the perks of being an older brother."

He turns to my desk to pick up yet more of his equipment, including various lenses that he

three

meticulously packs into his camera bag.

I don't bother to respond, instead I question, "You on the same flight back home as me? All set for the wedding of the year? I guess they have roped you into doing the photography."

He shrugs one shoulder, zipping up his now full bag.

"I'm happy to do it for the lovebirds, any girl who can tame Jake's dick deserves to look like a million bucks on her wedding day and have those memories captured perfectly."

"Will you be finished with your work here in time or are you heading back with me after the weekend?"

I empty my pockets on the other side of the desk, pressing the button on my laptop to bring it to life.

"Nah, I'm done here, got a shoot booked in New York for fashion week, then another the week after that in The Maldives. It's tough being me."

His lips curl up in a self-confident smile.

"Yeah, I guess it is."

Just as I plop myself in my chair, someone knocks on the office door and Zoey, one of my bar staff, pops her head in.

"Sorry to interrupt boss," she smiles over at Isaac knowingly, "Halle from last night wants a word."

She speaks to me but never takes her eyes from my brother.

He looks over at me, waiting for my response so I roll my eyes dramatically, knowing full well he's tapped most of my staff since he's been here, even some of the men.

I look back at Zoey, who is still eye-fucking Isaac and clear my throat to gain her attention.

"Bring her through, Zo."

She drags her eyes away from the object of her lust and gives me a cursory nod before slipping back out of the door and letting it close softly behind her.

"I wish you wouldn't fuck all my staff." I huff out, not looking at my brother but opening up my email application.

"I haven't fucked *all* of them Li-Li, just the hot ones."

Before I can reply, he's already at the door, camera in hand, "I'm off to take some pretty pictures, fancy a beer later?"

I take my eyes away from the email containing my flight confirmation details and nod my head once, "Yeah, I could do with a drink, I'll catch up with you in an hour or so."

Giving me a small, three-fingered salute, he leaves me to stare at the offending email. My mind numb at the thought of flying home, even if only for the weekend.

A brief and timid knock on my door drags me from the fog inside my head and Halle's auburn tresses appear in the now open doorway.

"Zoey said it was okay to come and see you."

three

She seems unsure and a little shaky but maintains eye contact with me, unlike the pitiful creature she was last night.

I smile to try and put her at ease and beckon her in, "Please, take a seat. How can I help you, Jinx?"

She walks slowly to the opposite chair, flicking her fiery hair over her shoulder as she begins to sit.

"I googled Jinx and watched a clip on Youtube, I don't mind having such a kickass nickname." Her smile transforms her face and brings life to her deep chocolate eyes.

"I would never dare give a nickname that wasn't kickass to someone who shares their name with a true goddess of our time."

Her cheeks flush, the rosy colour only serving to highlight her pretty face. I'm glad I've made her smile but hope she doesn't think I'm trying to chat her up or get into her knickers.

Silence thickens the air between us and she looks down nervously.

"Zoey said you might be hiring and maybe I could apply for a job?"

Her question startles me, this is not what I was expecting. I thought she had come in to say thanks for last night or to tell me she was okay, not to ask for a job.

"So you're staying on the island then? I only ask as the position is temporary for the tourist season."

She picks at the polish on her nails before flicking her eyes to mine.

"Yes, I'm staying, the girls said I can crash with them until I find my own place and umm...Ian, the guy from last night, my umm...fiancé or probably ex-fiancé has already gone back to the UK and dumped most of my stuff, minus any money I had, with the receptionist at the hotel we were staying at."

"Wow. He sounds like a really good catch. It might not seem like it now, but it looks like you had a lucky escape, especially if he found it so easy to dump you in a foreign country without a penny to your name."

She wriggles uneasily on her chair, her whole face now aflame.

In a small, shaky voice, one so quiet I have to lean in to hear it she replies, "Yes, well, some people are exceptionally good at hiding their true colours. Sometimes it's not the people who change, it's that their mask has fallen off."

Her words cut me deep, but I fight the urge to let it show, slipping my own mask of many colours back in place.

"Get Zoey or Kayleigh to schedule you in for some shifts starting tomorrow. I'm away for a few days but will check back with you later next week to see if you like working here. If you do and if you fit in with the staff, the job is yours for the next few months."

Relief washes across her face, "Thank you, Liam, that's the second time in two days you've saved me."

Now it's my turn to blush, I'm barely managing

to save myself, I don't deserve anyone to think I saved them.

"Don't thank me yet, the hours are long and the club is always busy. Thank me after you've done your first shift and come back to do your second. It's good to have you aboard Jinx, head out and see the girls to collect your uniform and get all the details."

She stands and then surprises me again when she walks around my desk and places a soft kiss on my cheek.

She doesn't stop or look back, leaving my office as quietly as she first entered.

"So who's the redhead?" Isaac asks while lounging on one of the sofas that overlook Aurora's breathtaking view.

"New staff member." My reply is curt and I don't bother to look his way.

"She's cute in a fiery, teeny whirlwind kind of way but man she's skittish."

My head snaps towards him, the words out of my mouth before I can stop them, "She's not a suitable conquest for you Iz, do everyone and yourself a favour and go fuck Mitchell from the kitchen, I've seen more of him tonight than in the last eighteen months."

He smiles, hiding it behind the lip of his beer bottle. "Easy Li-Li, I wasn't chasing the redhead, too nervy for me, besides I had Mitchell last night, I'm not looking for a repeat performance."

I snort, I actually fucking snort. "Well, you need

to tell him that because here he comes and I don't want to lose him, he makes wicked tapas, so go take one for the team."

Isaac looks over his shoulder at a fast approaching Mitchell, then looks back towards me, eyes narrowed, "Fuck you Li-Li, the guy is clingy, I don't do clingy. You know that."

I laugh as Isaac shifts in his seat, his once relaxed pose now tense.

"Now now, you could do us all a favour and let him cling for one more night, you're out of here tomorrow, problem solved."

He glares at me, his voice tight as he whispers 'He's got fucking awful halitosis man, I don't want that mouth around my…"

"Stop," I halt him, my shoulders shaking with undisguised laughter, "too much information." I look over his shoulder at Mitchell, who is only a stride away. "Incoming in five, four, three, two… Oh, hey Mitchell, have you met my brother Isaac? Okay, guys, I'm out of here, gotta pack for our trip tomorrow. I'll pick you up on the way to the airport, Iz. Enjoy the rest of your night."

With that parting shot, I'm up out of my seat and striding towards my office to hand over everything of importance to Rhian, who will be covering for me while I'm gone.

Isaac is going to give me so much grief for that little stunt tomorrow, but that'll teach him for shagging half of my staff and leaving me to pick up the pieces.

Besides, I haven't had so much fun in ages and he would do the same thing to me. That's brotherly love for you.

Well, it's the way Fox brothers love.

Hard, without limits, take no prisoners but loyal to a fault. Add some playful ribbing, lots of banter and you get somewhere close to the relationship we all share with each other.

Some days it's too much to take, others I need it like the air I breathe.

chapter 4

Liam

Home is just the same as it always was.

Filled with love, laughter and playful banter, yet it still manages to swallow me whole.

Maybe it's being the youngest of a large brood; my grandmother always told me that although I was the youngest, my eyes held emotions beyond my years. She told me my heart was beautifully unguarded and that my soul shone brighter because of it.

I wonder if she was still alive, could she still find my heart?

I've spent the last few years trying to paper over its cracks then burying it deep. Better to be vacant of heart than risk it being ripped from my chest, again.

I survey the scene around me. My mother is fussing over Jake's tie while he scowls playfully at her. My father is pouring his second snifter of whisky, even though it's not yet midday and my other

three

brothers lounge around cracking jokes with H, while trying to unsuccessfully rile Jake up about his impending nuptials.

We are all relegated to the ground floor of Jake's huge home, while Emma, Liv and Laura have taken up the first floor.

Catering staff and the wedding planner mill around us like ants, setting things up, making sure everything is perfect. Their jobs are made slightly more difficult by the sodden grounds. The weather, which has been atrocious for the last few days, finally abated, making today gloriously sunny but not sunny enough to dry out the lawn or the area outside the gazebo where Jake and Emma would soon take their vows.

With the clever use of some temporary decking and miles of lush carpet, no-one attending today would even notice the muddy puddles that still marred the rest of grounds.

Not that the Bride or Groom are worried in the slightest, I can honestly say that neither would bat an eyelid at getting married in raincoats and wellies, that's how happy they both are to finally commit themselves to each other.

Even a person so averse to love as I am can see the pureness that surrounds their relationship.

In unguarded moments, I almost allow myself to yearn for just a small piece of what they have found in each other.

Almost. Until I remind myself of what loving

someone with your whole heart can do to you.

"You'll go won't you darling."

My mother's soft words drag me from my thoughts and I pull my gaze away from the small army who are still busy transforming the gardens.

Clearing my throat, I look up into eyes so similar to mine and reply, "Go where? Sorry, I wasn't paying attention, must be jetlag."

H barks out a laugh, "Jetlag? After a four-hour flight? I think the littlest Fox has been burning the candle at both ends." He winks at me before taking the glass of liquor that my father hands him and downing it in one.

My mother frowns in H's direction, "Harry if you don't slow down I'll be forced to cut you off. You're full of enough beans without extra Dutch courage and I'd like to maintain the hope that your best man's speech isn't going to make me blush like a virgin on her wedding night."

A chorus of "Mother!" rings out from my brothers as my father throws his head back and laughs. H coughs and under his breath but still loud enough to hear says "You can't be on about Emma," which earns him a smack across the back of the head from both Jake and Josh.

My mother glares in his direction before refocusing her gaze on me.

"To the florist to collect the missing button holes, they only delivered four and it would be quicker to collect them than wait for them to send

three

more out to us."

I rise to my feet slowly, "Sure, does anyone have a car I could take or shall I just call a cab?"

"Take mine, the keys are hanging up in the kitchen, just before the garage door." Jake walks over to me smacking me on the back. "Thanks, little bro, I owe you one."

I look out at the rest of my family, all still playfully chatting, the excitement of the day filling them full of exuberance.

"Anyone else need anything while I'm gone?"

No one hears my question due to the laughter spilling around the room from yet another one of H's many jokes.

"Okay then, I'll be as quick as I can."

Not a single person notices when I slip away from the living room, out towards the kitchen. Grabbing the keys from the hook, I step into Jake's ludicrously large garage and walk with purpose towards his brand new Aston Martin DB7.

I run my fingertips reverently over the car's exquisite curves as if she is my new lover.

I've always wanted to know how James Bond felt behind the wheel of one of the most beautiful cars on the planet. I guess I'll give my brother's new baby a quick test run and find out. They won't miss me if I take a quick detour.

After driving around, marveling at the understated speed and agility of the Aston and pretending to be

007 for a short while, I pull up on the main high street, a few stores down from the florist. I almost don't want to get out of the car, the seats have molded to my body, cocooning me in an embrace both exhilarating and comfortable.

"I'll be back soon, beauty." I feather my fingers over the steering wheel in a gentle caress, then sigh loudly when I finally open the door to get out.

My thoughts are a million miles away from the task in hand, as I absentmindedly hit the door lock button and turn towards the direction of the florist.

All it takes is a fleeting glance of long, auburn hair to stop me in my tracks; my heart frantically bangs against my chest and my breath catches in my lungs.

About twenty feet away, walking towards me, is the one woman I wanted to avoid with a desperation that caused me to flee half way around the world.

She hasn't spotted me yet and I stand frozen, all thoughts of fleeing evading my mind when all I can see is her.

Her beautiful hair is even longer than before, reaching all the way down her back. Her face is the same pale cream and even though I am not near enough to see the freckles across her nose, I know the placing of every single one. She hasn't changed at all.

A plain white tee fits her small frame perfectly, the hem clinging to the waistband of her well-worn jeans, her trademark Converse on her feet.

three

It's only then I notice that she isn't alone; to her side, holding on tightly to her hand, is a little girl of about seven or eight. A little girl who looks nothing like the fire-haired woman beside her. This little girl looks like snow white; dark ebony hair frames a pale, round face with a deep pink smile tilting her lips. She's walking slowly, almost being reluctantly tugged along the street, yet nothing can stop her steadfast dedication of touching every lamppost they pass.

The closer they get, the more their resemblance becomes apparent when I get a flash of emerald green eyes and the hints of freckles across her pale skin.

If my heart initially stuttered at seeing her for the first time in almost three years, it is downright quaking at the realisation that this little girl is hers.

Her daughter.

After everything that happened between us, how did I not know she had a daughter?

"Liam...?"

Her husky voice, although tentative, pierces straight through my armour, straight into the depths of that deep hole where my heart still convulses in pain.

I lift my eyes from the girl, who is now happily running her hand back and forth over a railing, letting her fingers feel every bump of metal, up to her mother's surprised gaze.

The instant my eyes connect with hers, my foolish heart tries to break free of its bindings, willingly wanting to lay itself at her feet. I swallow down the need to touch her and whisper out a name I haven't spoken since the day she forced me to walk away.

"Cari…"

chapter 5

Cari

My mind goes completely blank.

Not the kind of blank where you forget to spell a simple word and try to wrack your brain for the answer, or the kind of blank where someone familiar calls your name to say hello, but their own name evades you. It's utterly blank, empty and devoid of any rational thought.

Not the typical reaction I get when bumping into one of my former students, but he isn't just a student. He is more, so much more.

In my world more isn't an option.

Wanting more only brings more of one thing, desolation and if there's one thing the last few years have been filled with it's just that.

I am lonely. So lonely that it feels like I'm drowning some days; drowning and yet I am surrounded by others who can breathe easily.

My loneliness doesn't consume them, only me.

Just seeing him, even as shell-shocked as he is to see me, fills my lungs with much deprived oxygen, forcing my blood to pump quickly around my veins and my nerve endings to burst back to life; the straightjacket of numbness loosening, my tired limbs prickling as feeling returns.

You see, I never felt lonely with Liam; he was my cure, my antidote, my elixir vitae. He pushed back the waters of loneliness almost to the point of drought.

I couldn't allow him to be that for me as my life is so diseased, so draining that I couldn't let him drown with me. So instead, I let him go.

No, that's not right, I pushed him away, I forced him to go.

I made out that what we shared was dirty, disgusting and wrong. I didn't just hurt his feelings, I annihilated them and in the process I pulled the oceans of loneliness around me, causing me to gasp for breath on a daily basis, as I flail around in their bottomless depths.

"Cari…"

My name on his lips comes at the same time as a sharp tug on my hand.

I blink up at him for only a second before the tug becomes more persistent and I struggle to maintain my footing.

three

Tightening my hand around Seren's I attempt to drink him in for just a few moments longer so I whisper in her ear, "Good waiting, Seren." hoping it will buy me just a few more precious seconds. I look back up at his face in time to see his eyes flick repeatedly from Seren, back to me, total confusion on his face, alongside a touch of hurt.

I swallow past the dryness in my throat, forcing out meaningless words.

"It's so good to see you, Liam. How are you?"

The greeting is pathetic and doesn't encompass a single thing that I truly want to say to him.

The tugging on my arm becomes more forceful and I lose my balance, stumbling quickly to remain in position. I should check that Seren isn't distressed, but I can't tear my eyes from his.

My stumble causes his eyes to once more stray from me to her, then back again. The light in his eyes dimming as he pulls the shutters down over his emotions.

"I should get going."

Four words that allow the ever-present drowning waters to submerge me once more.

He hesitates for only a second before side stepping us and walking away down the street, never turning to look back no matter how hard I stare at his form and will him to. I stare until he enters a shop a few doors away and keep staring even as the door closes behind him.

A sharp bite to the back of my hand causes me

to wince in pain and release my hold on her hand. With a speed I will never fully comprehend, she darts away from me towards the busy road and I have to propel my stiff limbs into action, grabbing her by the top of the arm, just as her foot reaches the curb.

"Stop, Seren. Please stop."

Four words that mean more than just simply stop or you'll hurt yourself.

Four words filled with desperation.

Four words that seem to fall on deaf ears.

She doesn't understand. It's not her fault.

She doesn't understand. It's not her fault.

My mantra said daily.

He doesn't understand. It was my fault.

A new mantra created just for today.

He doesn't understand. He doesn't know that thoughts of him are often the only things to get me through tough days.

He doesn't understand that I wish we could be…more.

He doesn't understand. It was my fault.

She doesn't understand. It's not her fault.

We walk home without further incident. The suffocating air of our small house starving my lungs of precious oxygen, yet filling hers and allowing her to breathe.

chapter 6

Liam

"What the hell took you so long?"

Isaac strides up to me taking the box filled with the replacement, Gerbera Daisy, buttonholes, out of my hands.

"Mother is having a shit fit, you've been gone two bloody hours and the ceremony starts in five minutes."

I shake off the emotional turmoil bubbling through my veins and give a one-shouldered shrug, aiming for nonchalance.

"I got a bit carried away driving Jake's new baby, you know damn well he'll never let me drive it again so I was just making the most of it."

My voice isn't quite as strong as I was aiming for, but thankfully he doesn't notice.

"Well, get your arse in gear, Liv has already been down twice to get this party started. It seems Emma isn't sticking with the tradition of the bride always being late. She actually wants to be on time to marry Jake and he's pacing a hole in the floor of the gazebo waiting for her."

He turns on his heels and strides out of the open French doors, towards the elaborately decorated garden, leaving me trailing in his wake.

The ceremony is just as I expected it; simple, understated and overflowing with the love the happy couple share.

I tried, I mean I really tried to enjoy it. I smiled in all the right places, clapped in all the right places and cheered the happy couple's first kiss.

I felt bad for not being more present, but my head and my bruised heart had been left on that pavement on the high street a few hours ago.

Left at the feet of a woman I thought I knew, yet evidently did not.

I force myself to eat the delicious food served at the wedding breakfast, even though it tastes like dust on my tongue. I laugh at the speeches, heckling H where necessary and I congratulate one of my best friends on marrying my brother.

All the while, my chest constricts and my limbs ache with the energy I am forced to use to keep myself under control.

To keep myself normal.

Every inch of my body screams at me to return

three

to that place and see if I can just catch a glimpse of her one more time.

To hear her voice. To not walk away.

To ask her for the answers I deserve.

To plead with her for forgiveness.

To beg her to let me be enough.

Why the fuck was I not enough?

So, she has a child. Did she think I would run?

Did she think I would ditch her after all we shared?

Yes. She did.

The bigger question, the one I attempt not to torture myself with is, who is he?

Who is the father of her child, the man she cheated on to be with me?

The man she chose to stay with.

It just doesn't add up.

I know Cari; I know her heart and she never showed herself to be a selfish, conniving, cheating, adulteress.

Then again, I'm hardly an expert. Maybe that's exactly who she is.

"Earth to Liam."

I look up from the beer that I've been nursing for the last hour to see Emma standing before me looking radiant, happy and more beautiful than ever.

"Well, if it isn't the new Mrs. Fox-Williams. Have you ditched your husband already for his more handsome, younger brother?"

Ruffling my hair like I'm her annoying younger

brother, she takes my hand in hers and pulls me to my feet.

"Mrs. Fox-Williams is my mother-in-law. I'll be Fox, just like Jake. You may call me Emma or Mrs. Fox but no more Jules. I'm a respectable married lady now."

Happiness emanates from her, like a beacon lighting up a starless sky.

I wrap my arm around her waist and lead her towards the dance floor.

"Well…since I've seen your knickers numerous times, Mrs. Fox is a touch formal and I'm not sure who this Emma you speak of is, so I'll stick to Jules. It suits you better and before you butt in, I kept my promise of not talking about your knickers in front of all these fine people, so the nickname stays."

Before she can reply I spin her out of my arms, then dip her towards the floor.

She looks up at me breathlessly. "I've missed you."

The truth of her words is like a sucker punch and my carefully constructed façade falters. Not one to miss anything, she latches onto my momentary lapse, cupping my cheek in her palm.

"You can talk to me you know."

I blink slowly, fighting the words that threaten to spill from my lips.

Clearing my throat my reply comes out as a hoarse whisper, "I know, I just…can't. Not today. Today is for celebrating. I'm really happy for you

Jules."

She kisses me gently on the cheek and we resume our slow dance across the floor. Just two friends, sharing a silence filled with more than any words would be able to express.

"Mind if I steal my wife back?"

Jake's voice comes from over my shoulder and I step away from Emma without releasing her hands.

"I think she's well and truly yours, bro. No stealing required."

Jake steps into my place, taking his new wife into a firm yet gentle hold. I don't bother with goodbye, yet I feel Emma's gaze on my back as I walk away.

I turn when I reach the edge of the gazebo and look back. The smile she gives me doesn't quite reach her eyes and I hate that my sour mood might dampen her special day.

With more strength than I knew I possessed, I blow her a kiss, pretending to catch the one she blows in return. A genuine smile lights her face and it's impossible not to return it.

Letting my gaze roam over the rest of the people in the room, I take in everyone paired up with their other halves.

My Mum and Dad dance together like they are the loved-up newlyweds, Liv and Nate look very much the same.

Josh sits with Laura in his lap, his hand gently rubbing her belly; I guess another announcement is coming soon, a new brother or sister for their little

Ivy who has only just turned five months old.

H and Isaac are propped up against the bar, shooting the shit no doubt.

Everyone is exactly where they are supposed to be.

Except me.

My mobile phone vibrates from the inside of my suit jacket and I take one last look at my friends and family before walking towards the side of the house and out onto the large gravel driveway.

I slip my hand into my pocket to retrieve my phone and the vibrations stop, letting me know that it was a text I missed and not a phone call.

Most likely Rhian from the club updating me on the last few days.

I swipe open my phone to call a cab and notice the text staring at me from the screen.

It isn't from Rhian.

I miss you.

This is the second time a woman has issued those words to me today, but this time they gut me.

I hesitate, my fingers itching to return the sentiment.

It is through a sheer force of will that I close the text and pull up a cab number, then hit dial.

The taxi dispatcher has to say her greeting three times before I can get the words out to reply.

"I need a cab to the airport, please."

three

I rattle off my requirements, then end the call, staring at the phone in my hand for the entire twenty minutes it takes for my ride to arrive.

My will gives out when I sit in the back seat, the quiet streets rushing past my window making me feel more alone than ever.

I miss you too.

We pull up outside the airport a short while later, the taxi driver waiting patiently for payment, but I am oblivious to my surroundings.

Even though the screen has long ago gone dark, I am still staring silently at it. Waiting, no, praying for a response.

"This is where you get out mate, that's twenty-five pounds, please."

I absently look up and catch his eyes in the rearview mirror. Clarity finally washing over me.

"I'm sorry, I forget to grab my bags. Can you take me back?"

He hesitates for a beat, "Girl trouble?"

I avert my eyes, looking out at the departure lounge before meeting his gaze again.

"Not a girl, a woman. *The* woman."

He nods once before checking traffic and maneuvering the car into a U-turn. When he's finally back on the road home, he mumbles under his breath, "Ain't that the worst kind."

chapter 7

Cari

I miss you too.

The reply takes almost an hour to come through. I don't even know why I sent the text in the first place; I never expected a reply.

I was sure his number would be different or, after our encounter a few hours ago, he would just ignore me. He has every right to.

So when my phone lit up with those four words I swear my heart stopped and all the air evaporated from the room.

Should I reply? Should I just leave it at that?

I let him know the words that are screaming through my head since I saw him earlier today. Maybe it's enough.

Maybe it's all I'm meant to do.

God, he looked good.

Older, of course, but no different; except for a

three

healthy tan and broader shoulders, he looked just like my Liam.

My Liam; only he wasn't mine.

I pushed him away in the worst way possible. With no explanations, no further contact and no apologies.

At the time, it felt like I was doing the right thing, not for me but for him. As the months passed and turned into years, the ache inside me that belonged to him grew and grew into this tangible being.

It walked alongside me during the day and it sat next to me during the long, painfully lonely nights.

My life wasn't my own. It wasn't fair to make him take on my burdens. He was too young to understand.

I tried; I really tried to convince myself all those reasons were valid. Some days it worked, most days it didn't.

I should have told him the truth, allowed him the choice in his life that I didn't have in mine.

The noise coming over the baby monitor pushes my thoughts away.

Seren is awake.

Her typical three hours of sleep has come to an end and soon she will be kicking at the sides of her bed, getting more and more upset until I go and get her.

As usual, I haven't caught up on my own sleep while she was quiet and now I face yet another long night, with a few minutes dozing if I am really lucky.

I pull back the duvet from my body, slip into my robe and make my way to her bedroom, listening as her kicking gets more insistent.

Opening the door, I'm greeted to the biggest smile I've gotten from her in days, maybe weeks.

If Liam's words stole my breath and stopped my heart, Seren's smile fills my starved lungs and kick-starts my frail heart, filling me with a warmth that pricks at my eyes and tingles in my toes.

Smiles from her are not rare, she smiles all day long, but smiles directed straight at me are like precious gems; blinding, full of magic and so beautiful you covet them.

In that moment, I want to pick her up and smother her in love. I want to squeeze her tightly and cover her face in kisses until she giggles and begs me to stop.

Instead, I take her hand in mine and guide her down the stairs. My instincts to love via touch and boundless affection would not be welcomed and despite knowing this, it still hurts.

My weary muscles are stiff, my vision is blurring from lack of sleep and my stomach churns with exhaustion. If I can make it through today, there is a light at the end of the tunnel.

Tomorrow is Sunday.

three

The one day of the week I get all to myself.

I can sleep, catch up on work and not worry about anything or anyone else, except me.

It is the day that Laura-Nel takes Seren and then stays overnight to give me a break.

While they go to the park, I go to bed.

While they play with jigsaw puzzles, I get my assignments ready for the week ahead.

Then, when Seren finally goes to bed, I get to spend a few hours with my best friend.

Laura-Nel has been my bestie since I moved from Wales when I was eight years old. She took one look at me, declared my accent was 'cool' and then told me I was her best friend forever. We have been inseparable ever since.

She comforted me throughout my father's death when I was eighteen. He was killed in a hit-and-run by a drunk driver and during those dark days she was a pillar of strength for both myself and my heavily pregnant mother.

Then, once Seren was born, she became like another daughter to my Mum. She was always over at our house, always helping me look after my sister while my mother worked nights.

My mother struggled a lot in the aftermath of losing him. She fought to keep the roof over our heads while trying to cope with the demands of a new baby and being a single parent, all while mourning the loss of her soul mate.

Laura-Nel helped us with no thought for what

she was getting in return.

Even during Seren's assessments and diagnosis as a toddler, she never walked away from us and became a crutch for us both.

That's why, when my mum passed away from a short battle with cancer when Seren was just three years old, I knew she felt the pain as keenly as I did.

It was our bond of both friendship and loss that forged our love into something unbreakable.

We were more like sisters than friends and Laura-Nel's home life meant she was eager to escape from the confines of an unloving home. She never suffered any abuse, just a complete lack of love. She often told my mother, yes told not asked because asking was not Laura-Nel's way, that she could adopt her if she wished. My mother always replied she already had, no paper was needed to prove it.

Without her, I would never have completed university and I would never have been granted the right to keep my sister.

She helped me fight to become her legal guardian as I struggled to complete my studies, all the while mourning the loss of the person I loved most in this world.

She put her own life on hold to help me rebuild mine and now that it is just Seren and I, she still supported us while trying to forge her own way.

three

My mother always laughed at me calling her Laura-Nel, you see her name is Laura Nelson but in our year at school there were three more Lauras so Laura-Nel was the name that stuck. She didn't just want to be another Laura, she liked her double-barreled nickname and always stood out from the rest of the crowd, dragging my new-girl arse along for the ride. Eventually, even my mother called her by it, despite the fact that she never met any of the other girls who shared her name.

Even as we fast approached the ripe old age of twenty-six, everyone still called her Laura-Nel; it suited her. Only now her name was said as one word, 'Lauranel'.

Laura-Nel, my sister from another mister, my saviour in more ways than one and the only person who knew about my affair with a student.

Did she judge me? No.

Did she tell me that what I was doing was wrong? No.

Did she understand when I ripped his heart from his chest and left it bruised and battered on the floor at his feet? Not fully.

Did she hate me for what I'd done, forcing me to listen to her opinion of how I not only broke his heart but also mine? No.

She was just there for me. Always there for me.

She saw my initial tears, she captured the following tears and she helped make my final tears stop.

She did this just by being her…and with copious amounts of tissues, ice cream and wine.

A good friend brings a bottle, Laura-Nel always brought over two.

I was dozing on the sofa when a sharp, laminated piece of card was forced into my eye. Shooting up from my slouched position, my eyes focused on the too close face of my sister, her hand still ramming the PECs symbol of a drink into my sleepy face.

This is her only form of communication; where we use words, Seren uses pictures.

"Okay, Okay, I'll get you a drink. Water or juice?"

Taking my hand and dragging me to the kitchen she threw my arm up in the direction of the fridge, indicating she wanted juice.

Seren might not have any words yet, but I've become an expert on communicating without them. She has quite a broad understanding of PECs symbols that she uses to request items, something that has taken us around two years to master. Otherwise, we communicate via a lot of body language and guess work, on my part at least.

It is the times when I don't understand her that things go awry.

When no matter what I think she might want, it

three

isn't the right thing, or those awful times when she's feeling unwell but has no way of telling me where she hurts.

Those are the times I can feel my heart break.

No, not break; it gets torn right out of my chest with a rusty pair of pliers, then squeezed dry until it is just a painful husk.

We might be sisters in the eyes of the law, but Seren is as good as mine. My child. My heart.

I love her, care for her, worry about her and put her above all else, even me. That makes her mine.

When your child hurts, you hurt.

When you don't know the reason that your child is hurting and they cannot tell you, you don't hurt, you bleed.

Think of being unable to say you have a headache or your tummy hurts, or that you have a toothache.

Think of these things happening to you but you cannot understand them enough to ask for help or even have the words.

It's upsetting, right?

Now, think of those things not happening to you but to your child.

I'm not sure there is a word to describe the level of fear, pain and desperation you feel at those times.

It is an agony too crippling to define.

This is my life now.

This is why I refused to burden him with it.

After getting Seren her drink, I settle her in front of her favourite box of puzzles and check the time on my phone.

2.15am.

I contemplate lying back down on the sofa for a few more minutes of rest when my phone flashes to signal another text.

It could only be him.

Hardly anyone else has my number.

Well, plenty of people have my number, but I can't count students, other teachers or the multitude of Seren's therapists as anyone who would text me during the early hours.

I'm not sure if it is exhaustion, hope or just loneliness that makes me open the message.

Or maybe it is need.

My selfish need.

Can we meet up before I leave?

Not what I was expecting. At all.

I need to be careful with my reply.

Nothing has changed in my life, but it is obvious his has changed significantly.

How much water can flow under a bridge before past mistakes are washed away?

I guess I owed him some closure at the very least.

I can meet today.

Keep it simple Cari, don't complicate things.

three

Our spot. Midday?

His reply was instant and the mention of our special place floods me with memories.

Yes

A one-word reply but I want to say so much more.

I vow to say all the things I should have told him before.

I will apologise, I will soak up his presence and then I will let him walk away.

Lying back down on the sofa, I stare up at the cracked ceiling that is in desperate need of a fresh coat of paint and close my eyes.

A few moments later Seren joins me, laying her full weight across mine and she begins to twist my hair.

She's not gentle in her ministrations but it still soothes me and I greedily keep my eyes closed so she doesn't move away.

When she finally pushes herself off my body and back over to her box of puzzles, I crack open my eyes and through the fog of tiredness, I watch a little girl content in her own world.

Content with a pegboard puzzle and a beaker of juice.

If only life could be so simple for us all.

chapter 8

Liam

She said yes!

I asked and she said yes.

Nerves bubble up inside me as I lie on my small, single bed, in my old teenage bedroom.

If I close my eyes, I can almost believe I've gone back in time to the era of our clandestine meetings and secretive texts.

I remember staying awake for hours swapping texts with her, often going to school the following day as a zombified version of myself.

Every word we shared was worth it, though.

Every moment spent talking to her is etched on my brain, creating a bittersweet film reel of our time together.

As much as it hurts to remember, I will never allow myself to forget that what we had was real.

I felt it. She felt it.

Until she didn't.

three

Until she felt nothing at all and I was left feeling too much.

Hours pass by in a weird state of anxiety riddled limbo.

I can't sleep, my brain will not switch off and flips from making lists of the questions I want to ask her, to the various scenarios that might play out.

Will she be truthful with me? Will she finally tell me why?

Will I get to touch her? Will I be able to lay my lips on hers one last time?

I glance at the luminous screen of my old alarm clock, wondering if the time it shows is correct. If it is, I have hours left to drown myself in my tortuous thoughts.

With a frustrated sigh, I kick off the comic book duvet that I refuse to allow my mother to throw out and forcefully propel myself out of bed.

Pulling on an old pair of athletic shorts and a too small t-shirt that I find abandoned in my bottom drawer, I quietly make my way out of my room and down the stairs; careful of every creaky floorboard along the way.

I spent months sneaking out to meet Cari at all hours of the night, so I've become an expert at avoiding the noise traps.

The house is still and utterly silent; everyone else is happily sleeping off their wedding induced overindulgences.

Making my way towards the kitchen, I'm surprised when I see a faint glow coming from beneath the door.

When I enter the large and impressive space, my eyes adjust to the dim lighting to find Isaac slumped on a barstool, his arms sprawled across the cold marble of the central island, his head uncomfortably positioned half on and half off one of his bare forearms.

He's shirtless, his legs still clad in his suit trousers and from this angle I can see part of an impressive tattoo across his shoulder blades.

I walk quietly around the side of the island, trying not to startle him and wanting to get a better look at his ink.

The closer I get, the more I can hear his heavy breathing; he's out cold. I'm betting his heavy slumber is a result of him helping H drink the bar dry. They both drank more than their share yesterday.

When I'm finally behind him I can easily read the words he felt important enough to make indelible.

Beautiful scroll lettering in a bold font runs across his skin.

Acceptance is Serenity

I guess my brother struggles more with who he is than I ever imagined.

It never crossed my mind that Isaac wasn't confident in his choices; he's always seemed so at one with himself. Something I've often envied and something I strive to emulate when I finally grow up.

three

We both share an artistic nature and we've always been tight. He's the brother I feel a deeper connection with and we have a bond of more than just brotherhood.

Even when we were small children, it was always Iz and me.

While Jake and Nate played sports and Josh spent hours with his head in books, Isaac and I would create fantasy worlds from any and all materials we could find.

Our creations littered our shared bedroom and often spilt over into the rest of the house.

I remember when we made the *Bat Cave* from papier-mâché, having collected weeks' worth of our father's daily newspapers, often before he even had the time to read them.

It was freaking awesome and totally worth the grounding we received for stealing those newspapers right out of the letterbox.

"Hey Iz, wake up Bro."

I give his shoulder a gentle shake and all I get back is an unintelligible grumble.

"C'mon buddy, let me help you up to your room."

Isaac and I used to share a room when we were younger but as everyone started moving out he claimed Nate's old room as his own.

"Iz, man, wake up would you."

I shove him a little harder and he wobbles precariously on the stool, finally causing him to stir.

"Leave m'alone, m'omfortable." His gibberish words make me force back a smile.

"Nah, you're not comfortable buddy, trust me, a nice soft bed will be a far better place to sleep this off."

"Mmm-hmm."

I take that as him agreeing to move and wrap my arm around him, all but pulling him up to stand.

His eyes open and he looks at me through his drunken stupor.

"Don't change Li-Li, don't ever change but don't stay the same."

I smile, his nonsensical ramblings, delivered like they are the most profound words of advice ever given, even manage to make me break into a grin.

"Okay, Iz, I won't."

"And, two, don't take shit, stand up for yourself because more often than not, no one else will."

He's completely serious so I nod and proceed to drag him through the kitchen, down the hallway and towards the stairs.

"And, three…three…fuuuuck, I forget… doesn't matter."

Through my chuckles, I more or less carry him up the stairs and reply, "I think that might be your most brilliant piece of advice yet."

We somehow manage to get outside his door

three

and he props himself up against it.

"I remember three-," he looks straight at me, straight into the depths of my eyes, "-laugh, at everything. You don't laugh enough anymore. You pretend."

With a slap against my face for good measure, he proceeds to push open his door and stumble to his bed, totally unaware of how his words have just affected me.

Before I can go to help him, he's flopped on his bed and passed out.

His words reverberate through my brain.

I know I pretend.

I also know it's time to stop.

Quietly closing his door, I make my way back downstairs towards the kitchen. This time when I enter I am completely alone; alone with just my thoughts.

In an attempt to give myself something to think about, I open the large fridge and scan the contents.

There are more than enough ingredients to make everyone a full English breakfast, something I'm sure they will all appreciate when they finally wake up. So I set about doing just that.

By the time I begin to plate up the mounds of bacon, scrambled eggs, hash browns and black pudding, I hear the sound of feet tentatively making their way down the stairs.

Moments later my mother enters the kitchen looking as fresh as a daisy, not a hair out of place.

She scans the feast I've spent the last hour or so preparing and gives me a warm smile.

"Someone's been a busy boy."

I hit the button on the kettle and set up the teapot.

Mum is a tea snob. No teabags for her, she only uses the finest tea leaves and likes to drink it so strong that it will put hairs on your chest.

I place her favourite mug in front of her and go back to making the toast.

"Couldn't sleep, thought I'd make myself useful and save you the job."

"Cooking for my boys has never been a 'job', it makes me happy. Although, I'm grateful for the help this morning. I'm feeling a little delicate."

I turn towards her, bringing the freshly made teapot and the tea strainer and placing them in the centre of the island, just in her reach.

Looking up at her face, I take in her features, from her smooth unblemished skin to her immaculately coiffed hair.

We got lucky with our gene pool. Both our parents have aged well.

"You don't look worse for wear."

She reaches for the teapot, lifts the lid and begins to stir the contents with a teaspoon.

"Well, I feel it. Wait until you see your father. I swear he toasted the good health of every single person at the wedding."

I smirk at her, setting a plate full of fresh toast

between the mountains of other breakfast delicacies.

"I think he was just celebrating the fact that there is a woman out there who was able to tame Jake's..." I want to say cock but settle for, "ways."

I give her a smirk and the knowing look she shoots back makes me certain she was thinking of the same thing.

A smile breaks over her face, "She's a special girl, my boy did good."

Knowing she loves Emma like a daughter allows me to return her smile with my own. It's impossible to not fall in love with 'My Jules' and the fact that her own mother isn't involved in her life means I'm more than happy to share mine.

"That she is."

Taking her first sip of tea and letting out a contented sigh, my mother locks her eyes with mine and I know what she's going to say next.

"So... when are you coming home for good? We miss having you here and I know managing one of Nate's clubs isn't your ambition in life. What happened to getting your art degree?"

I roll my eyes and turn back towards the hob to fry up some tomatoes and heat up some beans because Isaac refuses to eat bacon without baked beans.

"We've talked about this Mum, I'm happy where I am for now. In fact, I head back tonight."

Silence descends over us, with only the sizzle of the tomatoes breaking it.

I can hear my mother taking occasional sips from her tea but it is unlike her to give up so easily. I feel on edge waiting for her to continue.

Once the food is cooked and I have nothing else to distract my attention from the silence in the room, I turn slowly to find her staring at me intently.

"A mother loves her children unconditionally and without boundaries. She knows when they are hurt, she knows when they are happy and she knows when they are sad. She knows this without any words being spoken."

I swallow thickly yet still throw out my words as uncaringly as possible.

"Mum, please don't. I'm good. I'm happy, I swear."

"Don't lie to me, Liam." Her voice has gained strength but not volume. "Another thing a mother can tell is when she is being lied to."

I have no reply for that, so I stand and wait for her to finish, hoping she just imparts some advice and doesn't ask me any questions.

Not today. Today I might just break and spill my guts.

"Forgiving someone does not make you weak."

My eyes widen, not fully expecting her to go in this tangent.

"Sometimes you have to distance yourself from someone who's hurt you or you will never fully heal. Some people come into our lives and stay for a lifetime, others might only share a small chapter; only you know when it's time to forgive them and keep them in the past or allow them into your future."

I have no words.

None.

I keep my mouth sealed shut just incase my lack of words lead to an outpouring of others; ones I'm not ready to share.

Sensing my turmoil, she smiles gently at me and then turns her gaze to the food spread out before her, picking up a plate and loading it up with more food than I've ever seen my mother eat before.

Once she's satisfied with her overflowing plateful, she gracefully gets up from the chair and walks over to me plate in hand.

"I'm taking this up to share with your father, I'm bending my normal rules and letting him eat in bed. Life and relationships are all about compromise sweetheart."

Her soft hand strokes my cheek and I can't help but lean into her touch and the warmth that only a mother can provide.

"I. See. You. And if she's wise she sees you too. If she's stupid and doesn't know what she's let go, she isn't worthy of you anyway."

I can only nod in response.

"Now, let me go and feed your father. I'm hoping all this greasy food will soak up some of the alcohol in his system. If it doesn't, make sure your bed is made when you leave as he'll be sleeping in your room tonight."

Then she winks at me, pops a piece of bacon in her mouth and turns to leave the room.

"What if she is worthy? What then?"

The words croak out of my mouth in a painful burst.

"Then you compromise, sweetheart."

I spend the rest of the morning in my bedroom, clearing through my junk. I come across many of my old sketches and my chest seizes when I find the pencil drawing I made of Cari the first day we met.

I remember being unhappy with it at the time and I've never showed it to her. When she asked for my work at the end of that first day, I mumbled something about it not being good enough and hastily left her classroom.

Now, looking at my drawing, I see just how perfectly I captured her.

She looks serene, yet mischievous, young, yet full of wisdom and utterly carefree and beautiful.

The eyes that stare up at me from the paper are not ones that break hearts or hide away husbands and children.

They speak of hopes, dreams, life…love.

I fold the paper up and tuck it into my back jean pocket.

Maybe it's time to give her the final piece of my heart so that when I walk away for good this time,

three

she has the chance to offer it back; whole and not crumbled.

It's time to move on.

chapter 9

Cari

Seren and Laura-Nel left about an hour ago.

They are going to visit the aquarium where Seren will happily watch the fish for hours.

Before they left, I told Laura-Nel about my run-in with Liam yesterday.

After I picked her jaw up off the floor and then proceeded to tell her that I am meeting him today, she proceeded to warn me that it was not a good idea.

"Some things should be left in the past, Cari. Like shell suits and tie-dye."

Her insightful words of wisdom still ring in my ears.

I'm not sure whether her comparing my illicit affair with a student to some naff fashion trends was sheer genius or just utter rubbish. Laura-Nel always has a way at putting things into perspective.

Still, this is something I have to do and after I rolled my eyes at her daft comparison, I explained

three

why.

"He deserves the truth. I owe him the truth."

No more words were shared, she just kissed me on the cheek, zipped up Seren's jacket and after prompting her to blow me a kiss goodbye, they left.

Normally, I revel in the peace and quiet I get on a Sunday, but today the silence in our small home is deafening.

I pass the time with a quick shower and then spend the next half an hour pondering on what I should wear.

Does it really matter what you wear to see your ex-lover when all you're going to do is spill your guts and then watch him walk away?

Probably not.

I settle for my standard dark jeans, an old band tee and trusty red Converse. I might as well be comfortable.

I towel dry my hair, hastily braid it to one side and totally avoid putting on any make-up, not that I wear it often.

I'm sure it will look like I've not made any effort but this is just me. Liam knows who I am.

Well, he thought he did.

I don't want to mask the true parts of me that I always allowed him to see. He will never believe what I have to tell him otherwise.

I glance at the clock and see I have ten minutes to arrive at our meeting place. It's more than enough time to get there.

This place has always been ours.

When you're sneaking around, having an affair with a younger student and falling in love, you need to stay off people's radars.

Did I just admit to myself that I fell for him?

I look into the mirror mounted on the hallway wall, just before our front door and give myself a mental talking to.

I need to tell him the truth but not make it worse by telling him I loved him more than I should have, more than I deserved to and more than I ever allowed him to see.

That will only confuse things further and he does not need to know my feelings for him have not changed.

Seeing him yesterday only magnified those sentiments.

I loved him.

I still love him.

I make it there with minutes to spare and I take in the visual feast that is my father's allotment garden. A place I still pay rent on, maintain and attempt to grow veggies in and a place that is so special to me that I can never see me letting it go.

My eyes land on the scarecrow that Laura-Nel and I helped Seren make last week. I say, 'helped make', we made it while Seren did what she always does when we come here, she sits and watches the flowers.

She watches the flowers like other children watch the TV. Sometimes she brushes them gently, watching their petals and leaves quiver from her touch, sometimes she just watches the breeze ruffle through them and on rare occasions she may pull off a head and attempt to see what it tastes like. For that reason alone, I've researched what flowers are safe for human consumption and got rid of any that might cause her harm.

This place is as much Seren's haven as it is mine. Our back yard at home is small and barren. This allotment is lush and green, with rows upon rows of planted fruit and veg.

We even have a decent sized potting shed that my Dad built and inside are some basic amenities, like a small counter fridge and kettle.

It's this small but homely shed where things got out of control with Liam. This nondescript wooden structure housed many of our more forbidden activities and a blush begins to creep up my cheeks at the memories.

I guess the start of our affair began with something quite innocent. He spotted me one day, not long after he started my class, carrying bags of soil to the back of my car at the local DIY store.

He was there to buy some materials for an assignment I'd set the class. Their brief was to work with industrial items and turn them into something from nature, so when he saw me struggling, he offered to help.

It seemed harmless enough so when he also offered to unload them for me, I allowed him to accompany me to the allotment.

That day was the first of many.

That day was the start of it all.

Movement from behind me catches my eye.

I startle and turn to see him standing behind the main gate, looking unsure on whether to enter.

He looks just like the boy I once knew; a little quirky, a little shy, yet also filled with a quiet confidence.

His hands are pushed into his jean pockets and his shoulders are slightly slumped but the full weight of his gaze is fixed securely on me.

"Hi"

I break the silence and offer him a tentative smile.

"I'm glad you showed up, I wondered if you would maybe change your mind."

His eyes soften slightly and his shoulders give a small shrug, "I didn't know myself if I was going to show, but as you can see, here I am."

His voice.

God his voice.

Memories wash over me in waves, nerve endings

three

I long ago forgot about begin to awaken and I can't help the smile on my face from turning into a grin.

This is my Liam.

Now it's time to let him go and Lord forgive me, but I'm going to savour every single moment with him until I do.

"So, this is totally not awkward." My smile is shy and I look over towards him hoping to see him return it but his face is completely devoid of any emotion. I guess I deserve that.

"Shall I make us a cuppa, for old time's sake? I'm sure you have loads of questions and I'd be better prepared to answer them if my mouth wasn't currently as dry as the Sahara."

Still nothing.

I make the first move towards the potting shed and pull the keys out of my back pocket to open the padlock, all the while hoping he follows me.

Subtle warmth at my back lets me know he has and even though he's at least an arm's length away, my body reacts to his presence like it always has.

I fight the urge to turn around and look at him and work the padlock open, my fingers are uncooperative and stiff and the lock is fighting against me. Eventually, it clicks and I push open the door that creaks with disapproval. It feels like an omen and I shake off my anxiousness and step inside the small space.

The midday sun filters through the Plexiglas window, highlighting the floating dust motes that seem suspended in the air.

I feel just like one of those minuscule molecules.

Confused and comatose in my emotions; floating aimlessly just waiting for the slightest breeze to change the course of my direction.

When Liam steps into the shed, those particles floating in the air that so perfectly mimic the feelings inside me begin to move rapidly; constantly colliding with each other creating a swirling, unbridled energy that in turn, creates heat.

Heat I have no right to feel.

A quick check of the fridge confirms we have some milk and a quick sniff test confirms it's still fresh.

I grab the kettle and turn to go and fill it from the outdoor tap but before I can even move one step, a hand takes it from mine.

"Let me."

I flick my eyes up to his face but he's already moving, not allowing me to even get one look at his eyes.

Liam never could hide his feelings, even if he tried, it was always his eyes that would give him away and it seems he has learnt to guard even those from me.

I watch as he goes out through the door and see his form walk past the crack in the opening, around to the side of the shed where he knows the water tap is.

I stare at the empty space for a few moments too

three

long, then quickly distract myself by readying the mugs before he gets back.

When I feel him re-enter, I call over my shoulder, not bothering to turn and look at him "Milk, two sugars right?"

He places the kettle on the counter to the side of me only offering me a quiet "Please," before he exits the shed with two camping chairs in his hands.

Now I have the small space to myself, I can finally breathe again and the rapidly boiling kettle only serves to heighten my already frayed nerves.

Minutes later, two hot mugs of tea in my hands, I step out of the shed and back into the sunshine. The camping chairs that he's placed in front of it are empty and for a moment I think he's gone. A quick glance around the allotment and I find him. He's standing at the side of the scarecrow examining it like one would examine a piece of fine art.

If I wasn't so highly strung right now, it would cause me to laugh and possibly tease him but all I can do is watch and stop my feet from walking to were he is.

He, like me, seems to be able to sense when I'm around as his whole posture tightens and he stops his perusal of Worzel, (yes, Worzel, Laura-Nel named him of course) and walks back towards me, keeping his eyes lowered the entire time.

The words are out before I can stop them, "You can look at me you know, I swear I don't have Medusa-like abilities, you're not going to turn into stone."

He stops in his tracks, my remark catching him off guard and I have to swallow down a rapidly growing lump in my throat when his eyes finally connect with mine.

"No, maybe not but I swear I saw a snake slithering through your hair a little earlier, a guy can never be too careful."

His witty retort is delivered with a completely straight face and for a second I'm not sure if his words are in jest or not. Then I see his lip tremble slightly and a small curve fights its way to the corner of his mouth.

"Your face right now is priceless. No, you haven't got a snake in your hair, well at least not one I can see from here and yes, I'm just winding you up. You always were fun to tease."

That semi-smile transforms into a more obvious one and just like that all the tension leaves my body.

We can do this.

"Funny, Ha Ha. Come and grab your cuppa before I water the plants with it."

He does.

He takes his drink from my hand, sits in the camping chair next to mine and we talk.

chapter 10

Liam

"Why?"

The question slips out.

It's been burning on my tongue for the last ten minutes while we've shared a pleasant yet unimportant chat and skirted around the real reason we are here today.

I've barely paid attention to most of the prior conversation. Cari asked about my world trip, then quizzed me on my current job and completely avoided the topic of discussion that we should be having right now.

In fact, I think her last question was, "Are you planning on attending Uni in the future?", so when I answer her question with "Why?", I know I've confused her for a second.

I can see when the full weight of my question and it's meaning finally registers because her eyebrows scrunch together and a frown takes over her features.

She begins to fiddle with the hem of her old *Stone Roses* t-shirt and I want so badly to reach out and still her hands, to give her the comfort she needs to answer me, but I can't.

I can't because I need her to hurt to ensure I get the truth.

I need her honesty in its most raw and brutal form.

I don't fill the quiet that falls over us.

While I wait for her to speak, I take in every inch of her features, noting she hasn't aged a single bit.

She is still as strikingly beautiful as she was that first day we met.

I run my gaze over her face, down to the petite curves of her body, watching as her leg bounces nervously. It gives me a weird sense of comfort when I see a pair of red Converse on her feet, even if they are obviously a new pair. I can remember her ruining her old ones in this very garden the day we decided that a very muddy and wet afternoon should not hinder our ability to plant a new row of potatoes.

When my eyes trail back up her body to her face, I almost lose my breath as she has her dazzling, emerald green gaze trained on me, studying me intently.

"I want to tell you everything, Liam. Just please hear me out before you make up your mind about me. I know I've made some bad decisions but I made them with the best intentions. I never set out to hurt

three

you. I really need you to believe that."

I nod, unable to respond for fear of telling her exactly how much she hurt me and how much I've been hurting ever since.

She sighs and looks out over the allotment garden, her gaze catching on some new flowerbeds she must have recently planted.

"The year before we met was a tough one. Actually, it was more than that; it was the year to end all the tough years previously and I only just got through it."

She breaks her gaze from the flowers and looks back at me, letting me see the pain written all over her face.

"I'm not trying to be melodramatic. It's just the truth."

She shrugs, before again averting her eyes, a small smile plays across her plump pink lips.

"For eighteen years I had the best life. I had a life I took for granted, but then I guess everyone presumes that if we lead a good life, happiness is deserved, especially when we are teenagers."

Her hand moves to a gold chain around her neck before she runs her fingers underneath her t-shirt, pulling out a pendant that is shaped like a series of knotted hearts. She fiddles with it absentmindedly before continuing.

"My parents were in love, so in love it was infectious. They had the type of relationship most people never get to experience," her eyes briefly meet mine, "the soul deep, once in a lifetime kind of love."

The type we shared.

She looks away from me and a small laugh escapes her, "Some might say it was the sickeningly cheesy kind of love, they named me Cariad after all."

I know I shouldn't interrupt but I can't help it, I always thought she was just Car. My Cari.

"Cariad?"

She gives me her eyes once more and another small smile covers her lips while a slight blush forms on her cheeks.

"Cariad is Welsh for 'Love', I was born in Wales, lived there until I was eight, then we moved here for Dad's new job."

Cariad. It suits her even more than Cari.

"Anyway, I digress, my life was amazing…until it wasn't…and I didn't know what hit me."

Her eyes begin to fill with unshed tears and I want more than anything to soothe her but I need her to keep telling me her story.

She takes my silence as her cue to continue.

"The year my Dad died, I was eighteen. I'd just finished my A-Levels and was about to start University. To some extent I didn't just lose my Dad that year, I lost my Mum too."

My heart hurts for her and I don't want to let her think I don't care, so I lean over, unclasp her hands

three

and take one in mine.

"I'm sorry Cari."

And I am, but it still doesn't explain what happened between us.

She looks at our joined hands for a second, almost dumbstruck by my unexpected touch, then straightens her posture, clears her throat and continues.

"Mum was heavily pregnant when the accident happened, so my sister was born having never met him. She will never know what it's like to live in a household so full of love that you could almost taste it in the air."

Her smile turns sad, "We called her Seren, it's Welsh for 'Star'. Mum said if I was given to them as a product of how much they loved each other, then Seren was given to us to be our light in the dark. That she would be our guiding star during the bleakest of nights and Dad would always be able to find and watch over us because Seren shone so brightly."

At the talk of her sister her eyes gleam, filled with the love she has for her, illuminating her from the inside out. Unconditional love is reflected all over her features, truly showing how much of a joy Seren is in her life.

"Things were tough; Mum had to take on extra work as we no longer had my Father to provide for us. Add that to her inability to cope with her grief and a new baby and she became so distant I wondered if I'd ever get her back. Then…" she closes her eyes briefly, seemingly to compose herself, "then, when Seren started having difficulties she just shut down completely. She was in total denial. She wouldn't believe anything anyone told her about Seren and when she was finally diagnosed as having severe Autism at two years old, my mother just broke."

She wrenches her hand away from mine and frantically tugs the hair tie from the end of her long braid, running her hands through the strands before proceeding to re-braid it. The motion obviously calms her enough to resume talking.

"I remember the day she finally accepted it. Seren had been spinning the same toy over and over and over for about an hour, flapping her hands randomly and making funny noises of excitement. We were at another child's 2nd birthday party and all the other kids were playing on the bouncy castle or running around, jumping on all the soft play equipment and Seren didn't even know they existed. I watched as my mother would repeatedly move her gaze from the other kids playing, back to Seren. Over and over again, she looked between them then back to my sister and finally, I just saw it sink in. When we got home a few hours later, Mum put Seren in her room to play and I found her slumped outside her bedroom door. She had her head in her hands, mumbling the same thing over and over again. 'Please no, I can't lose her too, God no, please no.'"

She swallows thickly, her eyes glassy.

three

"A week later Mum was diagnosed with breast cancer. She had ignored the signs for so long that a full body scan showed it had spread. Actually spread was an understatement, it had taken over; very little of her body was unaffected. She fought for so long to stay with us but a little over a year later…she was gone."

Fuck.

How the hell did I not know all this?

Why didn't she confide in me, let me be there for her? The thought of her alone through all that makes my stomach churn and bile burns up through my chest.

That's when clarity washes over me.

"The little girl I saw you with the other day is Seren?"

My question shakes her from her thoughts.

"Yes. That's Seren. We had just been shopping for new shoes when you saw us. That's why she was so eager to get home."

Now it's my turn for honesty and I smile sadly at my admission, "I thought she was your daughter."

She looks at me intently before turning her head away yet again.

"She is mine. She might be my sister by title but I've been looking after her ever since. She's mine and she always will be."

Her words fill me with a sense of relief. I am overwhelmingly moved by her story and how she has struggled, but I still can't stop myself from feeling happy that she did not leave me because she had a husband and a child.

But if that's the case why did she push me away?

"I'm sorry." My words are filled with truth but seem completely inadequate, so I reach over and link my fingers with hers.

"I'm so sorry for everything you've been through but why didn't you tell me. I could have helped. I could have been there for you both. Why…did you push me away? Why did you let me believe there was someone else?"

Confusion, frustration and thinly veiled annoyance lace my final words. I don't mean to be harsh but I still don't understand.

This time when she turns to look at me her face is covered in both guilt and regret.

"There is someone else, can't you see that? I have someone in my life who needs me twenty-four-seven. My life literally revolves around someone else. I had nothing to offer you; the tiny piece of myself I could give to you was paltry in comparison to what you deserve. I *had* to let you go."

"No." I can't keep the disbelief from my voice, "No, I can't see that."

She stares at me dumbfounded.

"You pushed me away because you were trying to protect me from what? Your life? Your sister? You? What you fail to realise is you never gave me the choice. You never showed me everything you had to deal with, never allowed me to take some of that

three

burden, and I would have. I loved you so much that all this would never have been enough to scare me away."

"I know, and that's why I pushed you. These are *my* burdens..." her voices rises in intensity, "...I love...*loved* you too much to force them upon you."

I can do nothing but blink.

Blink. She loves me.

Blink. She still loves me.

Blink. She.

Blink. Loves.

Blink. Me.

chapter 11

Cari

Why did I agree to this?

Why didn't I just continue to deceive him?

Being this close to him is too much. Spilling my guts to him is too much.

I sound weak and whiny, moaning about my lot in life and offering it up as an excuse as to why I tore his heart out.

What I should have told him is, "It was just a bit of fun," or "I got bored and let you go," or "you were too young for me, it was a mistake and I used you."

Instead, I told him my entire, sorry, life story.

Hoping for what?

His forgiveness? His sympathy?

No.

I just want him to understand.

I want him to know I had good reasons for ending what we had, even if I've been nothing but an empty shell ever since.

I want him to know I loved him.

I still *love* him.

Not because I expect to fall back into his arms or for him to say, "Let's start again," but for him to have closure.

For him to know he is worth so much more and escaping me was the best thing that could have happened to him.

So when he just stares at me, speechless and blinking I can only do the same back. We stare at each other for so long that our blinks even synchronise.

Then that familiar pull that charges the atoms in the air seems to cover us and before I can form a rational thought, his lips are on mine.

He still tastes the same.

Like hope, like love, like Liam.

I allow myself to just float, like those dust motes in the sunlight. Lost in the millions of other specks that make up our universe.

I am lost; lost in us, lost in the feel of each other.

Our lips reacquaint themselves with soft caresses and light sighs.

We stand in tandem, both wanting to be closer to each other.

My arms wrap around his waist, his tighten around mine until there is no space left between us.

My air is his air.

My lips are his lips.

We are all touch and sensations, wants and desires.

We are us, not Cari and Liam, not two separate entities; this single kiss has made us one.

We break apart slowly and he rests his forehead on mine, eyes closed, breathing heavy.

"I've dreamt of you. No matter how far I've run, how many countries I've visited and how many breathtaking sights I've seen, it's only been you."

His words penetrate the shaky foundations of my resolve. This was not a goodbye kiss. I know that now.

This kiss was hello.

It was I've missed you, I've craved you, I've never forgotten you.

It was love.

Not a love like I had with my parents, not a love like I have for Seren, or even the love I have for Laura-Nel.

It was more.

Sometimes love can be explained as a kind of madness, other times a gift, there are even times when love can feel like a duty but this love, *this love* was life.

chapter 12

Liam

Kissing her is like coming home.

Her lips on mine breathe fire into my veins, light up my chest and melt something deep inside.

It hurts in such an exquisite way, exposing all of my dreams, all of my longings and all of the secrets inside me that have long lain dormant.

With her lips on mine, nothing else matters and yet everything makes sense.

"Soul meets soul on lovers' lips."

I whisper the words across her mouth before kissing each corner and causing her chest to rise with her panting breaths.

"Quoting Shelley is not fair; you know what it does to me."

I grin against her lips, "Sorry, slip of the tongue."

Her mouth opens with her light laughter and I take the opportunity to devour her lips with mine. Swallowing down her giggles until they turn into whimpers of need.

She pushes up onto her tiptoes to deepen our connection, her small, perfect breasts now smashed up against my chest, her lack of bra allowing me to feel her nipples even through the cotton of our shirts.

It would be too easy to get carried away in this moment; to pick her up, carry her into the shed, lock the door and strip her bare so I can worship every inch of her creamy skin.

My head, and my cock in particular, both scream at me to do so, but it's my heart that stops me. My heart is over-ruling my sex-starved dick and emotion-starved mind. It wants more than a quick fumble.

It knows this quick fumble could ruin me.

She senses the conflict within me and pulls away. My eyes latch onto her kiss-swollen lips and I fight with myself to gain some much-needed control.

"I want what you want…so badly I ache, Liam. But nothing has changed. No, that's wrong, everything has changed. You don't even live in this country anymore for starters."

I tear my eyes away from her mouth and stare into her emerald greens, it would be so easy to drown in their luminous depths, but I know she's right. This isn't how I wanted today to go.

"I know, you're right."

My words strike her like a physical blow and although she said it first, it hurts her to see me agree.

I never want to hurt her.

I never want her to hurt again.

three

She's had more than enough pain to last a lifetime, so I need to make this easy for her; I need to rip the Band-Aid off quickly and allow the scab that was once us, to heal.

"I leave tonight. I won't be coming back. There's nothing here for me anymore."

If I thought agreeing with her hurt, I can see these words literally flay her open.

I kiss her gently on the forehead, taking a deep breath of her scent into my lungs, trying to imprint all that is her on my memory.

"I have something for you."

I reluctantly unhook my arms from around her waist and pull the folded piece of paper from my back pocket.

"Just…don't open it until I'm gone."

She looks from the paper in her hand back to me, searches my eyes for a second and then gives me a small, sad nod.

"Be strong Cari, your parents gave you the perfect name; there is nothing in life that is stronger than love."

I press my lips to hers once more and keep my eyes open so I don't miss even a second of seeing her. That's how I see the single tear that escapes the corner of her eye and leaves a lonely track mark down the soft skin of her cheek. I want to kiss it away, to erase the evidence of her pain with my touch, but instead I take a deep breath, turn and leave her allotment garden without so much as a second glance.

Each step that takes me further away from her is like a bolt to my chest, causing my feet to grow heavy and my legs to ache like I'm physically carrying a ton weight on my back.

I force myself to keep going and even when I get back to Isaac's motorbike, which I borrowed to make the journey here, the pain in my chest doesn't lessen.

I straddle the seat of the KX Zephyr motorcycle, unhook the helmet from the handlebars and roughly push it on my head; it immediately restricts the air from getting into my already starved lungs and I know I have to get out of here quickly. I kick start the bike, flick down the visor of my helmet and scream away from the side street like the devil himself is chasing me.

I ride through the city, out into open countryside, allowing the scenic views rushing past me and the high speed of the machine underneath me, to dull the nagging ache.

By the time I reach home a few hours later, it's almost dark.

I lied to Cari about leaving tonight, I haven't even confirmed my flight back to Ibiza, but I know for the sake of my sanity I have to do it soon.

It hurts that she didn't beg me to stay, didn't ask for more even after our kiss, but then what did I expect. She told me she wanted to give me closure. I was just foolishly hoping for today to be our hello, not our goodbye.

I should be glad she finally shared the truth;

three

relieved she laid herself bare for me and gave me the answers to all my questions, even if I didn't fully understand them.

I'm not, though.

Seeing her hurt, knowing how hard her life has been just makes me want to be there for her even more.

I can't even begin to imagine what it's like to lose a parent, let alone both of them in such a short space of time and I haven't got the first idea of what it's like to care for a small child with Autism, but what I do know is I love her just as much as I did before. Probably more.

Can I let that love go knowing she feels the same way?

I pull out my phone and make a call, one that can't wait.

When she answers I don't beat around the bush with pleasantries, I just give her the facts.

"Rhian, I won't be back for a while, the club is all yours. If you need me you know where I am." She begins to butt in with questions about Nate, but I cut her off, "No, he doesn't know yet but I'll call him next. He'll be fine with you taking over for while. I have something I need to take care of and I'm not sure how long it's going to take."

Or if it can even be fixed.

"All the upcoming events are scheduled on my planner, use my office if you need to. I'll see you in a week or two."

Before she can question me further I hang up.

I know that was unprofessional of me, but right now I couldn't give a shit, some things are more important.

Now, I just have to wait for Cari to make the first move.

In order for us to stand a chance, she needs to be the one to initiate things. I need to know she not only loves me but is willing to fight for me.

Love; just a four letter word that is easy to spell yet impossible to define.

I may need her to prove I'm worthy of fighting for, but for her, I'm all set to go to war.

chapter 13

Cari

I sit staring at the piece of folded paper in my hand, the fingers of my other hand skim lightly over my lips that are still tingling from his caress.

A kiss that initially felt like hello soon turned into goodbye and I'm so bloody tired of goodbyes.

I flick my eyes over the garden, from Seren's flowerbeds to Worzel the scarecrow and back again to the paper I absentmindedly stroke between my fingers.

I wonder if this seemingly unimportant sheet that has been folded into quarters, contains the words that will forever tell me goodbye.

This thought is the reason I hesitate to open it. If I never open it then I can pretend it's not true, so I gently smooth out the creases and place the paper in the back pocket of my jeans.

It only takes me a few minutes to wash out our mugs and lock up the shed. Now Liam has left, I don't want to stay here alone. A place that has always given me comfort, even after I pushed Liam away, now feels barren, despite its overabundance of produce that is ripe for picking.

I lock the entry gate and slowly stroll back towards our house, hoping that Laura-Nel and Seren are back from their aquarium visit.

Normally, I relish these few hours of me time, but today I can't think of anything worse than being alone, stuck with my own thoughts, replaying every second of the short time we just spent together.

Opening the front door, I am met with silence.

"Laura-Nel…Seren…you guys home?"

My voice seems to echo in the empty house and for a second I am tempted to turn around and go straight back out, but where would I go?

Instead, I pour myself a cold glass of water and head towards the small room I use as my office-come-studio.

A blank canvas sits on the easel in the corner of the room, calling to me. It beckons me, asking me to use the bleakness I feel filling my veins, wanting me to pour it all over the crisp, barren surface with paint.

Slipping off my Converse and jeans, I place both by the door and pull on my painting overalls.

When I get consumed by my art, I totally let go and paint has a tendency to cover whatever I'm

three

wearing at the time, so the overalls have become a necessity.

I load up my palette, grab my brushes and focus my feelings.

Then, I paint my melancholy in fine brush strokes, using all the colours of the spectrum to purge my sorrow, my anguish and even my guilt onto a canvas that once was bare but now contains the darkest recesses of my heart.

Hours later, I stand in front of my completed work.

I reach out to touch the shadowy figure that sits just off centre, almost consumed by gloom and my fingers itch to bring that person back into the light.

The figure is content to sit in darkness and just watch as the bright sunlight pours through the open window, the breeze encouraging the sparkling, free floating, dust motes to swirl in reckless abandon.

I'm not sure if the figure is him or me and I'm not sure if we long to be those particles of freedom or if we are just waiting for the opportunity to shut the window and bring calm to the chaos inside.

"Hey, Cari, you home?"

Laura-Nel's voice calls from the other side of the house, shaking me from my intense perusal of the image I've just painted.

I quickly set down my materials, strip off my

overalls and head out to meet the two most important people in my life.

"I'm in my room," I call out as I open the door, "Did you guys have fun with the fishies?"

I walk down the hallway towards the living room just in time to see Laura-Nel hanging up their coats.

She has a sparkle in her eye that tells me they had a great time at the aquarium and I'm instantly jealous I missed out.

"Don't freak out okay, but I think Seren said a word today, well at least it sounded like a word and afterwards she kissed me."

Laura-Nel beams as she fills me in on the milestone I've missed. My stomach cramps with the knowledge I've missed something so important, at the same time my heart soars in the hope that this actually happened.

Tears prick at my eyes, but I swallow quickly to keep them at bay.

"W…what do you think you heard her say? Was it like any of her other sounds? What were you doing when she said it?"

I fire the questions at her rapidly and she just smiles and grasps my shoulders with her hands, bending slightly to look directly into my eyes.

"Breathe, Cari."

I inhale then exhale slowly a few times and then open my mouth to grill her less hurriedly. As my lips form shape to speak again she closes me off, "I heard you the first time. If you can just stop freaking out on

three

me for a second, let me get Seren set up with her juice and puzzles and I'll fill you in on every detail, okay?"

I give a light sigh and force my shoulders to relax, "Okay."

We walk together into the living room and Seren has already set herself up with her iPad. She would happily spend all day on it if you let her, but I try and limit her and vary her activities or else you can never move her on to try new things.

She doesn't even look up when we enter, not that I ever expect her to anymore but feeling a little emotional has made me hope that just once, *just today*, she would.

Laura-Nel heads into the kitchen for her juice and I sit on the floor next to Seren, looking over her shoulder at the Mandala app she has running on the screen in front of her. It plays soothing pan pipe music while the screen in front of her changes through a kaleidoscope of colours and patterns, allowing her with just one touch of her finger, to change the design or the way it moves.

It's mesmerising and totally calming, so I greedily use the opportunity to scooch closer to her, allowing my arm to brush hers and my hand to rest against hers on the floor.

My heart stops in my chest when her fingers snake out to curl over mine and it takes all of my control to remain unaffected.

Laura-Nel walks back into the room and her eyes

immediately land on our joined hands. A warm smile takes over her face as the telltale shimmer of tears fills her eyes.

She doesn't speak, just sets Seren's beaker on the table in front of us and then sits on the floor on her other side.

Seren keeps my hand in hers and allows Laura-Nel to sit equally as close as I am.

The three of us are content in this rare moment of comfort.

If there is one thing Autism has taught me, it's to take even the smallest, seemingly unimportant things, the moments that to someone else would be part of everyday life, and cherish them.

For us, there is no such thing as small.

Every event, no matter how insignificant, is bigger than I can ever describe.

Nothing in life is, or can ever be, taken for granted and just like that, the ache inside me, the loneliness I felt watching Liam walk away, slowly lessens.

No, it will never completely go away and yes, I will always carry it with me, but this house where touches are precious, affection isn't shown in ways that are typical and words are rarely used to convey feelings, is filled with a love so pure, it's often blinding.

Who needs to be a speck of dust when you are someone's entire world.

"Come and have a cuppa with me in the

three

kitchen."

Laura-Nel's softly spoken words break the spell that surrounds us and Seren quickly removes her hand.

I place a swift kiss on the top of her head, barely laying my lips on her hair and follow my best friend.

Clicking the kettle on to boil, she turns and rests herself against the worktop, looking at me from head to toe.

"Judging by your lack of clothing and paint-spattered hands, either today went well and there's a half naked boy in your studio or it went badly and you're painting away your frustrations. Which is it?"

I roll my eyes and grab the chocolate biscuits out of the cupboard. This talk requires copious amounts of dunking and chocolate digestive biscuits are the best dunkers ever.

"He's not a *boy* and he's definitely not in my room. I'll fill you in on my day as soon as you tell me what you think you heard Seren say."

The kettle boils and Laura-Nel quickly makes our tea, placing my steaming mug full in front of me a few moments later.

"Well, we had been looking at the same bloody fish tank for over an hour and I wanted to move her on to more interesting things. The one she was obsessed with didn't even have many fish in it, I swear she was just transfixed by the bubbles."

She grabs the biscuits, slowly sliding a few out before placing the packet back in front of me.

"And?"

"Cool your boots, let me get some chocolatey goodness in me and I'll keep going, don't panic."

One dunk and an entire biscuit in her mouth later and she continues to talk, but with mouth full of melted chocolate her words come out garbled.

"Anyway, I'm trying my best to entice her onto the next set of tanks but she kept wiggling out of my grasp and bouncing back over to her favourite, which was the utterly boring one. When I bend down to talk to her I swear she told me 'Sws' then placed a smacker on my lips. Isn't sws what your mother always asked us for when we were younger? I'm sure I remember her saying 'Come and give me a big sws.' Then giving me a huge smacker across the lips."

I stop, a chocolate biscuit is mid-dunk in my mug of tea and soon breaks off, melting into squidgy mush and sinking to the bottom of my cup.

"You've lost your biscuit." Laura-Nel helpfully points out.

"Stuff my biscuit, what exactly did the word sound like? I want you to repeat it *exactly.*"

"Well it sounded like 'sooooossss' and like I said, I got a kiss after it. I didn't imagine it, Cari, I promise, but maybe it's just a new sound of hers."

I shake my head, "It's not a new sound, I ask her for a sws every night before bed. My mum always asked me for one every night before bed…my father always asked me for one…" my voice cracks and I feel Laura-Nel's hand on mine in an instant, "…it means kiss. She was trying to distract you by asking for a kiss."

"You'll hear her say it, I know you will."

I look from where her hand rests on mine, up to her face, trying and failing to contain my overwhelming emotions.

"I'm sorry, it's just been one of those days, you know."

She pats my hand, grabs herself another biscuit and aims for nonchalance when she asks, "So, I got me a sws today, it's about time you told me if you got one too…and I don't mean from Seren."

My fingers reactively touch my lips, my mind replaying what we shared.

"Judging by the non-answer and the goofy look on your face, I'm guessing some lip action happened today, so stop holding out because I'm not bathing Seren for you until you fill me in and you know she has a tendency to strip, we don't want a mess in the living room now do we."

I can't help the laugh I blurt out, "Great, I'm on the 'spill your guts before Seren begins to finger paint the living room and not with paint' stopwatch am I?"

As soon as the words are out of my mouth, we both glance at each other and realise that she has been very quiet in the next room.

Springing to our feet, we both rush into the living room and find Seren exactly where we left her on the floor, clothes and the all important nappy are still in place, her focus still on the iPad in front of her.

"A-men for Steve Jobs I say."

Shocked Laura-Nel even knows who he is I turn towards her with a questioning look on my face.

"What? Didn't think I knew him hey? Well, how could I not when the holy hotness that is Michael Fassbender is playing him in a movie. That man melts the knickers straight off my arse."

The snort that comes from me is so loud and unladylike, even Seren looks in our direction before going straight back to her iPad.

"Trust you!"

She looks at me with a 'who me?' expression on her face.

"Hey, a girl needs her obsessions," she inclines her head to Seren, "it just so happens mine are hot men and dirty books, which coincidentally work in perfect harmony with each other. I can combine them so when I'm reading my dirty books, I can also visualise the hot men I've done hours of previous research on and thus, my life is complete."

She looks at me, waiting for me to be in awe of her genius.

I arch a brow at her, "Hmm, that and the B.O.B. you keep in your bedside drawer." Her mouth drops open and she starts to interrupt, but I hold my hand out to stop her. "I know it's not a torch and leaving it out next to one of your dirty books kind of gave the game away."

She tries and fails to look embarrassed, "And no,

three

it's not a page counter, bookmarker or any other contraption you might try to fob me off with."

She rolls her eyes, "You're right, I'm busted, it's my reading companion. B.O.B. is a literary connoisseur who particularly likes both fictional and factual stories and accounts of human sexual relationships."

I snort again, only slightly quieter.

"You mean he likes," I shake my head at the stupidity of talking about her vibro like it's a real person, "what the hell am I talking about? *It* is not a he...you mean *you* like erotica."

"I mean *we* like erotica." She winks at me.

"It would probably do you good to..."

I shoulder nudge her to stop talking, "*Do not* finish that sentence, I'm quite happy with the books I read, thank you very much."

She scrunches up her nose in distaste, "Yeah, books by old blokes about love. Sounds sooooo much fun."

Before I can try to explain the virtues of reading Shelley, Keats or E.E. Cummings she's already half way up the stairs to run Seren's bath, calling over her shoulder as she goes, "Don't think I've forgotten."

"Forgotten what?" I call after her.

"That you still haven't told me about what happened today. I've already got a bottle of wine in the fridge and you will tell me every single detail later. Moscato always loosens your lips."

Then she's gone and I hear the bath being run.

Seren is still immersed in her iPad and with Laura-Nel's words reminding me of Liam, I pat my backside looking for the back pockets of my jeans. The fact that I'm standing here in my *Stone Roses* t-shirt and knickers, having left my jeans on the floor of my studio, tells me just how pre-occupied my mind currently is.

I grab my jeans from the floor of my studio and rifle through the back pockets until I come across the paper Liam gave me earlier.

Walking back towards the living room, I internally debate with myself about opening it up to read the words that will undoubtedly tell me goodbye. Instead, I make my way across the room to sit by Seren on the floor.

Before I know what's hit me, she's snatched the paper out of my hands and torn it in two within seconds.

"No, Seren!"

My stomach lurches but I manage to get the two halves from out of her hands before she causes any more damage.

"Naughty! That was naughty."

She doesn't even look at me and I don't have the heart to tell her off further. To her, it's just paper and paper sounds good when torn. It's as simple as that.

Quietly getting up from the floor, I gather the torn fragments of paper and bend to lay a light touch on her hair. "I'm just going to fix this, okay?"

three

Typically, I don't get a reply but I don't need one. I am just letting her know what I'm doing; trying to fix something that is broken beyond repair and I don't mean the paper in my hands.

Taking the pieces over to the small bureau that sits in the corner of the room, I open the latch, pull down the front and lay out the sections on the old, scarred wood. Then, opening a drawer, I find some tape and slowly place the pieces face down.

Written in scrawled writing on the back are the words 'I remember when I saw you for the first time.'

Before I fix the tear with tape I turn over the wrinkled pieces and place them together.

Staring up at me is an exquisite pencil drawing of my face.

Only it doesn't look exactly like me, it looks like a younger, more carefree, more beautiful version of me.

Like I've been airbrushed and all my worries have been taken care of, illuminating my eyes from within.

The girl looking up at me from the paper is effervescent and full of life.

Even torn, this artwork is truly breathtaking and I feel tremendously guilty that I allowed it to get damaged; I also feel elated that this is how he sees me.

Liam has always been talented and looking at myself through his eyes brings the ache in the pit of my stomach back full force.

My chest feels tight, like it's about to rip open and everything that could be and should be mine, stares up at me in shades of grey lead.

Swallowing down my emotions, I turn the paper back over, hiding the soulful eyes that stare too deeply into my heart, but the words that are there burn themselves into my brain as I gently tape the two halves back together.

A choked whisper leaves my lips once the task is complete, "Remembering is the problem, it would hurt less to forget."

chapter 14

Liam

I wake the next morning with a renewed sense of purpose.

A quick phone call to Nate yesterday secured me some time off and my mother was ecstatic when she found out I'd be staying home for a few more days, plus…I have a plan.

I want Cari to come to me, but that doesn't mean I'm going to sit back and idly wait for her.

I'm going to remind her daily of what she gave up, what she misguidedly threw away, but she still needs to be the one to fight for us, even if I'm providing her with ammunition to do so.

Straight after my shower, I make a few phone calls and have an important appointment booked for later on today. It gives me more than enough time to search through my old portfolios and select another piece of art to send to Cari.

This time, I chose one she's seen before.

It's a pastel drawing of her allotment garden. One I created the day after we finally gave in to the desire between us and the day I gave her what I had yet to give anyone else; my heart.

Not just my heart but also my mind, body and soul.

I was quite a popular guy in school but kind of a late bloomer, so I never messed around with girls the way some of my friends did.

That made Cari my first…and my last.

I've tried to meaninglessly hook up and get her out of my system, but when it came down to doing the deed, I just didn't want to.

It wasn't that I couldn't, my cock certainly cursed me a few times for not being allowed to get off, it was that my head and my heart would always scream at me to stop, despite my body practically yelling at me to let go.

So there has only been her.

Sometimes it feels like there will only ever be her.

That's why I have to see this through.

She might not see it yet, but together we are stronger; together we can take on anything life throws at us.

I want to be the one who stands by her side with her hand in mine during the tough times, who holds

three

her close and soothes her fears during the dark times and who laughs, celebrates and dances with her during the best of times.

I want all of it…but only with her.

Placing the pastel image into a plain folder, I grab a Sharpie and write along the front 'Remember this day, this perfect day? Life wasn't complicated then, it doesn't have to be complicated now, in fact, it's quite simple; you find what it is that makes you happy and who it is that makes you happy and you're set. That's perfection. – I hope you find it again.'

I seal the folder, attach a note to the front with her address on, hoping she still lives there and by the time I've taken a quick shower and got dressed, my Mum is calling up the stairs, "Liam, there's a courier at the door for you."

I grab the folder and head downstairs, meeting my mother's curious gaze when I get to the front door.

"Work for Nate?" she asks with a quirk of her eyebrow noticing the folder I have in my hands.

"No, something more important." I give her a light kiss on the cheek and move past her to the open doorway and to the motorcycle courier who is patiently waiting to deliver my package.

I hand over the folder, sign for payment, thank him quickly and close the door.

My mother still waits for an explanation, but I just smile and shake my head, "Curiosity killed the cat. Wasn't that one of Grandma's favourite sayings?"

She huffs lightly but her reply is full of humour, "Your Grandma also said that self-love would make you go blind. I have five boys with 20/20 vision, so I think it's safe to say not all her words of wisdom are worth taking notice of."

I groan at her in mock embarrassment, "Mother, do you have to?"

She wraps her arm around my shoulder and guides me towards the kitchen, "Fair's fair, wouldn't you say. Besides, I didn't come out and say anything about masturbation; you came to that conclusion all by yourself."

My next groan is genuine, "It's no wonder this family is crazy with you at the helm."

She squeezes me tightly before letting go and heading towards the fridge to make breakfast, "After all you boys have put me through I'm allowed to be a little bit cuckoo. It's actually a wonder I have any sanity left. Now, do you want a full breakfast sarnie or muffins?"

Isaac strolls into the room and answers for me, "We'll both take a full brekkie please Mum," he walks over to give her a good morning kiss and adds, "then Li-Li here can come over to my studio and give me a hand with some framing."

Downing a full glass of orange juice, I wipe the back of my hand across my mouth before answering, "Li-Li is busy, find another slave."

Turning in my direction, he gives me a quick wink before sitting across the counter from me, "Oh,

three

I wasn't looking for a slave. I'm not sure that would be an appropriate position for you, given we share blood and anyway, I currently have a few prospects vying for that role."

The devilish glint in his eyes is all for my mother's benefit and she takes the bait, smacking him across the shoulders with her tea towel.

"I will not have any of my boys into that M&M or M&S or whatever they call it funny business. Just find a nice girl or boy to settle down with and then go and get freaky in private, without the whips and chains."

We both laugh until tears form in our eyes but clueless to her words, my mother just stands there not getting what we find so funny.

"What? What have I said now?"

Choking out the words through my residual laughter I enlighten my mother on her faux-pas, "M&Ms are sweets and M&S is where you buy your underwear, I think the acronyms you are looking for are S&M or BDSM. Neither are appropriate breakfast conversation, Mother."

Then it's her turn to wink, "Oh, my boys, I just like seeing you blush. I've read *The Story of O*, I'm not as vanilla as you lot might think."

Her shock admission causes tandem groans of mortification from both myself and Isaac, but luckily we are saved from further embarrassment when my father enters the kitchen.

"Morning, what is everyone groaning about? Did

I hear someone ask for ice cream for breakfast?"

The three of us look at each other trying and failing to maintain a straight face, Isaac breaks first. "Dad, can I just say I admire you, you're my hero for putting up with Mum for so long."

That earns him another whip from her tea towel, but my father just looks lovingly towards her, "Trust me, she's my hero. I'd be lost without her."

There is only sincerity in his words and all joking stops to be replaced by a feeling of rightness, of home.

Knowing what Cari has endured the last few years and knowing how lonely she must feel, not only makes me fully appreciative of what an amazing family I have, but also makes my heart ache that she doesn't have this kind of support in her life.

My family is often crazy and sometimes infuriating, but there is nothing more secure than being surrounded by unconditional love.

The rest of the day passes quickly and soon the time comes to set off for the appointment I made earlier.

Before I can leave I need to send Emma a quick text; I've already cleared the reason for the visit with her, but I've been deliberately vague about the details.

She and Jake are currently on some paradise island celebrating their honeymoon, so I don't really want to intrude on their time together no matter how important this is to me.

Just heading 2 the school we talked about this morning. Thanks 4 agreeing 2 work with me on this

Her reply comes through just as I jump into the back of a taxi and give the driver my destination.

I'm excited 2 find out more. This is an area I've wanted 2 get involved with & Jake is fully behind us. Keep me posted.

I reply with a thank you and around ten minutes later I pull up to the secure gates of our local special needs school.

The sign above reads 'Welcome to Trinity Waters School & Resource Centre' and below, 'Please announce arrival via intercom.'

I thank the driver, pay the fare and step out in front of the gates.

Pressing the button to speak I clear my throat of any residual nerves and when a pleasant voice comes over the speakers I introduce myself.

"Hi, I'm Liam Fox, I called this morning to discuss a grant with the Fox Foundation and for a tour of the facilities."

Moments later, a jovial-looking man in his early to mid-fifties comes out to greet me. He shakes my hand so vigorously while thanking me for my time that I feel my whole body quake with the movement.

After going through a strict identity process and being provided with a visitor's badge, the Headmaster, Mr Thomas, who shall henceforth be known as Shaky Hand Man, shows me around.

"We cater for a wide range of disabilities and special needs within the school, from Cerebral Palsy to Severe Learning Difficulties, from Downs Syndrome to Autism. Our classes have a mixed range of children and as you will see when we visit some, the children are grouped by stage and not age, so you may see some ten-year-olds in the same class as our five-year-olds."

A lot of what he tells me is totally foreign to me and my limited understanding of special needs, so I begin to feel like a fraud; that is until he takes me to some of the specialist rooms they have within the school. We pass through various sensory rooms, a large therapy pool and then on to a half-finished space he calls a 'Rebound therapy room.'

"As you can see, this room is unfinished at the moment due to a lack of funding but we are hoping to raise enough to complete it by next spring."

I look around the space, taking in the trampolines sunken into the floor and the thick padding surrounding the walls.

"This room will help with everything from physiotherapy, to play therapy and will be an important addition for the children. Once this is complete, our next task will be a new integrated art

three

studio."

Before he can speak further I interrupt, "What if I could get you the funds to complete both? How long would it take before the children could access it?"

I know I might be giving him false hope by suggesting I could possibly get enough money for such a huge project, but I'm sure I can convince Jules.

He looks at me, mouth gaping slightly and shock evident on his features at my proposal.

"Well...if the funds were made available quickly, it would take about 6-8 weeks to complete both."

I nod and give him an encouraging smile, "I need to present the required donation to the board, so if you could email me costings and some information on the benefits that both new additions will have for the children, I'm sure I can persuade them to move quickly."

The smile he gives me is nothing short of astounded.

"That would be...well, it would be life-changing for some of our children, Mr. Fox."

I grow a little uncomfortable at his praise, I do have another less noble reason for my visit and so I deflect his grateful declarations with a question.

"Can we see some of the classrooms now?"

"Of course, of course. Can I ask why you decided to volunteer your help to us today?" He then rethinks his words and adds quickly not to offend me,

121

"Not that we are not extremely grateful, it's just we find new donors often have some link to the special needs world, a friend or family member maybe?"

He's hit the nail right on the head and I use the chance to grill him about something I need desperately to know more about.

"I have a...friend who has a child with Autism. I wanted to find out more about it so I could fully understand what families and individuals with the condition have to deal with on a day to day basis." I look over at him ruefully, "So you see, my motives are not entirely altruistic, I was hoping to pick your brain. The information I found on the internet was confusing; lots of talk about the triad of impairments, the spectrum and other information that completely went over the top of my head."

I think I blush at my admission, but Mr. Thomas just takes it in his stride.

"I think it's admirable you want to find out more. Your friend is very lucky to have you." He gives me a knowing smile and adds, "If we take a tour of the classrooms, we can then head over to our ASD or Autism Spectrum Disorder provision and I can try and give you some easier to understand information on what is a very complex and diverse condition." He motions me to go through the door ahead and continues, "I've worked with children with special needs, including Autism, for over twenty years and the best piece of advice I can give you is when you've met one child with Autism, you've met *one child* with

Autism."

I turn back and look at him in obvious confusion.

"What I mean by that, Mr. Fox, is *all* children, those with and without Autism are unique. What affects one, might not affect another, add to that the very nature of Autism and it being a spectrum condition and you will never come across the exact symptoms or challenges in each child. It also means the severity and complexity of how it affects someone varies drastically."

My face must fall with disappointment, my lack of understanding evident and he rushes to add, "But, I can help put the broader terminology you read on the internet into more perspective and hopefully, by the time you leave here today, you will have an increased understanding of a very complex condition that is often very difficult to understand."

I spend the best part of four hours at Trinity Waters. I meet some truly inspirational children and some equally inspirational staff members and true to his word, Mr. Thomas educates me on all things Autism.

When I leave I am by no means an expert, but it has clarified my understanding.

I even get a glimpse of Cari's sister in one of the sensory rooms.

It didn't enter my head, when I booked the

appointment this morning, that she would attend this school. Being the leading provision in our area for Autism interventions, I guess it's quite obvious in hindsight, she would be a pupil.

When we enter the dark room, I am immediately struck by the gentle vibrations that I can feel in the air and the calmness that comes over me.

Seren is lying with her face pressed up against a bubble tube and the carer who sits next to her, looks up at me and smiles when we enter the room.

"The tube is her favourite; the colours, the bubbles and even the vibration from the motor calms many children, just as it's calming Miss Seren here."

Mr. Thomas' hushed explanation of the scene we've intruded on gives me ample to time to watch the little girl that is the centre of Cari's world.

She doesn't move except to occasionally run her cheek up and down the tube's smooth surface.

The silence is broken when her carer gives her a five-minute warning that her time in the room is almost over. I watch enraptured as she uses a small traffic light looking timer to begin the countdown.

Mr. Thomas explains, "Seren is a very visual learner, she knows when the timer reaches red, it's time to go." I keep my eyes trained on the little girl with ebony hair and familiar emerald green eyes.

Her carer joins in our conversation, "Seren knowing it's time to go and Seren wanting to leave, are two very different things. Some days she will leave with a smile on her face, others she doesn't

three

understand why she can't stay longer and then we have a bit of a fight on our hands."

Mr. Thomas takes those words as our cue to leave, but I struggle to stop myself from watching the little girl whose eyes are now flicking from the changing colour on the timer, back to the bubble tube in quick succession.

"Can Seren talk?"

I'm not sure why I ask the question, I guess it's to gain further insight into Cari's life. I should feel guilty about asking, but the little girl we just left in that room is crowding my thoughts.

"We class children like Seren as pre-verbal; at the moment she doesn't have any identifiable words, but here at Trinity Waters we don't like the term non-verbal, we like to hope all our children have the capacity to use their voice when the time is right. She, like a lot of our children with severe Autism, communicates in other ways. You remember the picture exchange system I showed you in one of the classrooms?"

"The small symbols with the words on them?"

He smiles in approval that I was paying attention and replies, "That's the ones. Well, Seren uses those to request items such as toys, food and drink. So she does have a voice, it's just not one you can hear with your ears."

I nod again, storing it away with all the other bits of information I've gleaned from today's visit.

When we arrive back at the reception area, I turn

to take one last look at the school; a place that in a few short hours has crept its way into my heart.

Turning to face Mr. Thomas, I reach out my hand to shake his, "Thank you for giving up your time to show me around today; I appreciate all the information you've supplied me with and I'm sure the Fox Foundation board members will be just as keen as I am to support you in your upcoming projects."

He beams at me and vigorously shakes my hand again, this time with even more exuberance "The pleasure is all mine."

No sooner than I am out of the door, I begin to text Emma, determined to keep my end of the bargain.

Today has been a revelation and at no point during the day did I feel overwhelmed by the information I gained from my visit.

If anything, it makes me even more determined to show to Cari her life does not scare me off. In fact, I want to be part of it even more; No matter how tough things may be I know I am capable of not just being in her life but also helping to ease the burdens she faces.

Together we will be stronger.

School is amazing! U need 2 visit when U get home. The kids are inspirational & there are loads of ways we can help

This visit has opened my eyes in more ways than

three

one.

I think I've finally found the path I'm supposed to take, one that leads me straight to Cari but also leads me to fulfillment.

chapter 15

Cari

The next day brings more memories of Liam.

The breathtaking pastel scene, delivered by a courier this morning, is one I've seen before, but the effect it has on my heart is no less potent.

It also makes me wonder if he's still here, still in the country, just a few minutes away from where I sit now.

The words that accompany my gift speak of perfection and I am awash with memories of the day this beautiful artwork depicts; it was just that, perfection.

It was the day I allowed all my fears and worries about my emerging feelings towards him, to evaporate.

They floated away on the warm summer breeze the very second his soft lips met mine.

I knew my actions would have consequences, but in that moment I couldn't fight it anymore.

three

The then eighteen-year-old Liam consumed my every thought with his passion, his vulnerability, his honesty and openness.

With him I felt like Cari; not the Cari who hadn't slept for weeks or the one who had spent the previous few hours scrubbing shit off the TV screen from where Seren had taken her nappy off and finger painted everything she came into contact with. Nor was I the Cari that was still paying off her late mother's funeral bills.

With him, I didn't grieve or worry.

I didn't feel a loneliness so powerful that it often crippled me. Neither did I cry myself hoarse with my fears for the future.

He made me the Cari from *before*.

The person who loved, who lived and who had dreams of the future so colourful and vivid, she painted them daily so she would always have a record of them.

I liked finding her again.

I liked being her with him.

That day was perfection, not only because it was the day we first made love, but it was also the day I allowed myself to get caught up in his hopes and dreams. The day I believed we had a future together, despite the age difference and the fact that I was his teacher and despite the responsibilities I had at home.

It was perfect.

Until it wasn't.

Until I had to rush from his arms because

Seren's nursery had called and I'd missed it. I'd missed it because I was too busy lying naked in his embrace; the sounds of our lovemaking drowning out everything around us.

While I reveled in the feel of his sweat-slicked skin against mine, she had got so upset during her nursery session that she badly bit another child; one who's only fault was to try and hug her when she was upset. Then, during the ensuing meltdown, she head-butted the floor so hard that the staff had to take her to Accident and Emergency with a gash on her head from landing on a discarded toy.

That day showed me bliss was temporary and that my actions not only caused pain to the little girl who needed me the most, but it would also cause pain to Liam, eventually.

The trouble was, I already loved him; I'd already jumped in with both feet and no matter how hard I tried to stop it from going further, I always succumbed to his unconditional comfort, his youthful joy and his soulful hazel eyes.

I wasn't strong enough to give him up and in the end my choices only served to cause even more pain.

I reverently place the image of the allotment garden on my desk. My fingers skim over the spectrum of muted colours and a sigh unconsciously leaves my lips.

It's typical of Liam to give without needing to receive anything in return.

I'm just not sure why he's choosing to remind

me of what we had when he rightly walked away from me yesterday.

Maybe he's just reminiscing before he finally closes the door on our past for good. Maybe he's purging us and what we had from his system.

I hope with all my heart that in the future he will only remember the good times and not that final day when I pushed him away so horribly. If I close my eyes I can still see his face and the devastation that I caused reflected deep in his eyes. I don't blame him for running; I hurt him so completely and so thoroughly he felt the need to leave all his hopes and dreams behind in his quest to escape.

If I could have escaped, ran away from myself, I would have; so I had no right to question his decision to do the same.

My classes go smoothly; it's currently summer break so I only have a few voluntary, community college students who are building up their portfolios in the hopes of applying to art schools around the country.

During term time, I work part-time at a local secondary school and I still work two nights a week at the college.

Although I'd love to take on a full-time, permanent position within a school, this schedule allows me to be there for all of Seren's needs.

She goes to school while I work during the day

and Laura-Nel stays with her for the two evenings a week I have my college classes.

Today I have less time for my students as Seren is at a holiday play scheme her school provides. For a few hours a day during the long, summer break, they take her to allow her to have the consistency of a routine she is familiar with and I can use the time to help some of my more talented and conscientious students.

I arrive at Seren's school with a few minutes to spare and stand within the entrance vestibule, waiting for her to be brought out to meet me.

A few other parents are also waiting and I give them all a polite smile, but my attention is caught by a conversation coming from the reception desk, the name Fox immediately putting me on alert.

"Did you see him? He's just as hot as his older brother, I wonder if he's an actor too?" a high pitched female voice comes from just out of sight. The answering voice is again female but sounds more mature.

"Stop being inappropriate, Shelly. He's here on behalf of the Fox Foundation not for you to drool over," the voice chastises.

"Oh don't be such a party pooper, it's not often we get celebrities visiting, especially not ones who look like him." The younger voice giggles.

three

"His brother is the celebrity, not him and don't let Mr. Thomas hear you talking about him that way; that young man has pledged to help us raise thousands for the new rebound room *and* the art room. The last thing he needs if he visits again is you fawning all over him…even if he is as cute as a button."

I can hear the laughter in the older woman's voice and the responding shriek makes me smile. I catch the eye of the man opposite me and he rolls his eyes in mock despair at the conversation we have all been listening in on.

My brain doesn't get the chance to fully turn over all the words I've just heard because coming through the main doors, holding onto the hand of Mary, her one-to-one carer, is Seren.

Today has been a good day; I can see that by the smile on her face and the way she skips and bounces through the door, her eyes landing on mine for a just a spilt-second before she averts her gaze and heads in my direction.

"We had a great day today, didn't we, Seren?" Mary says as she hands me her school bag.

I take Seren's hand in mine, thank Mary for taking care of her and we make our way out of reception. As we approach the school gates, a figure on the other side of them gets into a taxi that waits at the curb. For a split second I swear it looks like Liam.

The car pulls off before we get close enough to get another look, but just one glimpse has me flustered.

Seren has stopped at the same place she does every day, a wire link fence. She likes to run her hand over the metal grid the fence forms and I always let her, even if only for a minute; sometimes it's easier to acquiesce to certain things in order not to create unnecessary conflict and if it doesn't cause anyone or anything harm and it brings a smile to Seren's face, then I let her do it.

As I stand and watch her, the conversation I overheard inside the school replays in my head.

"Stop being inappropriate Shelly, he's here on behalf of the Fox Foundation not for you to drool over."

Clarity hits me full force and my head snaps up in a futile attempt to look for the car that has long gone.

It was Liam.

He was here.

He hasn't left yet.

We walk the rest of the way home without incident, my mind full of questions that only one person has the answers to.

Twice I pull out my phone to text him, but both times I get no further than opening up my contacts and looking at his name.

I have no right to be part of his life in any shape or form; I threw that right away when I told him I loved another more than I could ever love him. I led him to believe I used him and that I had someone else.

three

What he didn't know was the someone else I needed to be there for, who I love with my whole heart and who deserves to be the centre of my world, is the little girl holding my hand.

chapter 16

Liam

Day three, post-kiss and I'm buzzing with electricity.

I wake with a renewed energy flooding my system and it sizzles through my veins demanding release.

This is a feeling I've missed.

The *need* to create, the *need* to visually express what my words cannot.

I'm giddy with this feeling, skipping a shower and breakfast to head straight to the room I long ago commandeered as mine; well half mine.

What once was our old toy room, then our games room, gradually became an art studio and photography room.

Under a silent agreement, Isaac and I stole this room right out from under our brother's noses and made it ours.

Judging by the neat way everything is stored away when I get there, indicates that Isaac has no need for this space anymore and my mother has cleared it up and left it waiting for us.

Old cameras line the shelves on one side, the dark room door is wide open and it looks like nothing has been touched in ages. On the opposite end of the space, my easel stands like a proud but lonely figure, long forgotten and highlighted by the sun streaming through the skylight directly above.

Paint splattered drawers run along the nearby wall, containing everything from acrylics, to watercolours, pastels, to graphite pencils.

This was my haven.

The place I poured my dreams onto paper and my heart onto canvas.

Gathering all my supplies, I find a blank canvas stored in the cupboard and excitedly place it upon the easel.

Over the next few hours, I paint the vision from my thoughts.

Flowers, trees, birds, butterflies and falling leaves surround the image of a woman and a small girl walking hand in hand. The girl is reaching towards a butterfly that dances just out of reach, a beatific smile on her face, while the woman is reaching for an outstretched hand, the owner of which stands just out of view, but is close enough that their fingers touch.

Once dried, this will be Cari's next gift.

I don't want to send her another memory; I want to send her a glimpse of what could be.

"Who's the girl? The one you ran away from?"

I jump at Isaac's words, having not heard him enter the room.

"Fuck, Iz, a little more warning please," I wave my brush around his face,

"I could have used this as a deadly weapon and poked your bloody eye out. What good is a one-eyed photographer?"

He ignores my question, his eyes fixed on the drying canvas.

"I'm guessing she's married with a kid or a single mother? Makes sense why you ran. Never knew you had a thing for older women Li-Li."

I nervously begin to clean my brushes, not wanting to spill the truth. Not wanting to admit I had a torrid affair with my art teacher and that she then dumped my childish arse by leading me to believe there was someone else.

He shocks me out of my thoughts once more when he places his hand on my shoulder and squeezes.

"Is she why you stayed, why you're still here now?"

I can give him this so my reply is easy, "Yes."

He nods and then his lips quirk into a smile, "Well then, I love her already."

I huff out a laugh, "It's as simple as that, hey?"

His face turns serious and he replies, "It's as simple as that."

He goes to leave, but my words stop him, "What

does your tattoo mean?"

He stops dead and visibly tenses. For a few seconds, I don't think he's going to respond but then in a voice more vulnerable than I've ever heard come out of my confident, older brother he replies,

"Everyone deserves to be accepted Li-Li. Both for their strengths and their weaknesses; for who they are and who they want to be, but first you have to accept yourself. Don't look for someone to complete you, look for someone who accepts you completely."

He leaves the room without waiting for me to reply. His words hang in the air long after his physical presence has gone.

Can I get Cari to accept me, to accept us?

Can she trust me enough, believe in me, *in us* enough, to see that I accept her and everything that comes with being part of her life?

Acceptance is serenity.

I accept all that she is and all that comes with loving her, I just hope she gives me a chance. *Gives us a chance.*

The painting is still tacky hours later and I know I won't be sending it to Cari tonight.

Instead, I call Emma; I text her first to make sure that interrupting her honeymoon isn't going to get me into trouble with her possessive new husband.

"Hey Jules, how's paradise treating you? You

sick of Jake yet? I can arrange flights out in the morning if you are."

"Watch your mouth, funny fucker. Being my blood won't be enough to save you when I get home." Jake's growl comes over the speaker before Emma laughs and interrupts, "You're on speaker, Liam. Jake wanted to say Hi."

I can hear what sounds like a kiss, then Jake's voice booms louder than before, "Keep this brief, I'm taking my wife to dinner. You have until I get out of the shower to take part in your girlie catch up and then I'm cutting you off."

The sound gets muffled and then Emma's voice comes over the line clearer than before.

"Ignore him, he's just miffed that Nate and Liv are flying out in a few days; although why he's miffed when he arranged and paid for their flights, I don't know."

I chuckle into the receiver, "My big brother never was very good at sharing."

I hear the sound of running water before a door closes and then Emma states, "I'm all yours. Is this about the donation to the local special needs school?"

I flop down on my bed, trying to gauge exactly how much I want to divulge during this conversation. "Yes, I wish you could see the place, Jules, it's such an inspiring environment. The kids, the teachers, they just blew my mind. Kind of put a lot of things into perspective for me and I really hope we can help them as much as possible."

three

"I'm sure we can Li, but I have to ask, this came right out of the blue. What made you go there in the first place? I mean, I'm excited to get involved, but I thought you'd be back in Ibiza by now."

And there it is, the question I hoped could be avoided.

"I just...well..."

I can't find the right words.

If I confess why I initially went there she might think I'm a stalker or worse, a saddo, who refuses to believe this thing with Cari and me is over.

"Liam, you're talking to me, the girl who spilled her guts to you in an Italian bar, remember? I think it's time you did the same. We can either have this talk now, or when I get back, but something is eating you up and has been for a while. Besides, I'm your sister now too, I get to interrogate you when I think something is wrong."

I rub my eyes with my free hand and let out a heavy sigh, "If I tell you, you can't judge her for her choices. What we had was consensual, she didn't corrupt me, she's not even that much older than me."

"I...I don't understand. One minute we are talking about you visiting a school, the next about some mystery woman you think I'm going to hate. Just start from the beginning and I promise to just listen, no judgment here."

So I do; I spill the story of a boy who fell in love with his art teacher even when they both knew it was wrong.

A boy who gave his virginity to his teacher and in doing so he also gave her his heart.

When I finish, I tell her Cari's final words to me before I packed up and travelled the world

"I can't love you, Liam. I don't have enough room in my heart for you. It is full to bursting with love for someone else, someone who needs me more than you ever will. We should never have happened. I used you to escape. I don't love you and you are too young to love me. It's over. Don't contact me again. Don't think of me again. Just go, live your life and follow your dreams because they can never include me."

She is utterly silent.

"Jules, are you still there?"

She tries and fails to sniff quietly, then the croak in her voice gives away her tears. "Don't cry for me Jules, it's not as cut and dry as it sounds. There was nobody else. She got some stupid idea in her head that pushing me away was saving me from something. In her mind, she really believed hurting me was the only choice she had."

Her voice is hushed and she tries to keep control of her emotions when she replies, "I still don't get it, Liam; you don't hurt someone you love. She deliberately hurt you, there's no excuse for that."

"There is if you think that small hurt will be saving them from a lifetime of it. I don't agree with her decision and it still pains me that she discarded me…but I understand now why she did it."

I then tell her everything Cari shared with me the other day.

The loss of both parents, her sister's diagnosis and how she fought to be her carer and finally how hard life is for her as the single parent of a child with severe autism who has no family support.

"That's why…" her voice is no less emotional when she replies, but she doesn't seem as hurt by my fucked up love story.

"That's why, what?"

"That's why you went to the school…"

I'm hesitant to confirm it, but I can't lie to Jules, "Yes, but not to stalk her or anything, I didn't even know it was Seren's school. I just wanted to get some information about Autism, some tangible information, not the gobbledygook you find on the internet."

"Oh, Liam…"

I close my eyes and wait for her to continue, to tell me I've overstepped an invisible line, but what she says makes my breath catch.

"…the kindest people are those who have felt the most pain. Only you would seek out the answers to better understand the life of someone who others would deem has wronged you. The same way she seems to have sacrificed her chance at happiness, to give you the opportunity of a life without the burdens she carries. She wasn't saying goodbye to you, she was saying I love you."

I knew she would get it; I knew she wouldn't judge and would see my actions and also Cari's, for what they were. Done with the best intentions, done out of love.

Clearing my throat, I smile, "I knew you'd understand Jules, you're the smartest person I know, now just tell me what I can do to make her fight for us. To make her see we are worth taking a chance on."

"I don't have the answer to that Liam, but if being apart has made her half as unhappy as it has you, my guess is she just needs her eyes opened a little. Show her the man she has missed out on loving because...*you* are one of the most amazing people I know."

"I love you, Jules."

"Love you right back, Li. Now go get her tiger."

My laughter bursts free, "Tiger? Have you been reading those tacky romance novels again?"

"No, if I had, I would have said, 'Go get her stud.', besides...you're more tiger-like."

The deep voice of my brother comes from somewhere in the background, "Why are you calling my little brother a stud? Do I need to kick his arse again?"

We both laugh and I can hear Jules blowing me a kiss before saying goodbye, her last words still make me chuckle even after we hang up, "C'mon over here husband and show me that alpha-maleness I married you for."

three

I'm happy my best friend married my brother, but I can also admit to being a little jealous.

Tomorrow I'll take a leaf out of Jake's book; tomorrow will be the day I show my alpha-maleness.

I just hope Cari doesn't mind hearing my tiger roar.

I roll my eyes and laugh, cursing Jules for ever using those words. Hours later I'm still humming that blasted, catchy *Katy Perry* song, right up until my mother joins in, adding some animal sound effects for good measure.

You know it's time to retreat to the safety of your room when you've made your mother roar.

chapter 17

Cari

A whole day passes without any more gifts from Liam and I finally believe he has returned to his job overseas.

Not receiving anything from him yesterday leaves me feeling empty and even though I refuse to admit it to myself, I want this communication between us to continue.

I want it so much that despite Seren sleeping well last night, I tossed and turned in bed, unable to switch off my thoughts.

Today is going to suck; I'm so bone tired I may just fall asleep at my desk during my summer school class. Not that it should embarrass me anymore as I've certainly nodded off with my eyes open quite a few times over the years. Lack of sleep will always strike you down when you least expect it.

I get through my day without incident and without falling asleep at my desk. The hours fly by

three

and it's soon time to collect Seren from her summer play scheme.

She's having another great day and I even get an unprompted kiss when I pick her up. If I wasn't so tired, I might have had the energy to savour it more, but it does bolster me through the short walk home.

Not long after I've settled Seren in bed my phone chimes with a text from Laura-Nel, letting me know she's outside. She knows not to knock just in case it's loud enough to disturb her.

When I open the door to my best friend, she's wearing a beaming smile that almost splits her face and has a bottle of wine in each hand. At her feet is a large box, wrapped in brown paper.

"I come bearing gifts." She says while handing over both bottles and proceeding to pick up the box at her feet; a box I can now see is larger than I originally thought.

"You moving out? What's in the box?"

She shrugs, while struggling to maneuver it into the living room, "How the hell do I know, I found it on your doorstep," adding excitedly, "Open it. Open it!"

I eye the box warily, trying to disguise the frantic beating of my pulse and the overall feeling of hope that pours over me.

It must be from Liam.

"Bloody hell Cari, don't just stare at it, open it! It's not going to bite you...oh, hang on...I've seen *Seven*, what if it contains *Gwyneth Paltrow's* head?" She kicks the box, jumping back when something inside tumbles over.

"Fuck! It's alive!"

Her melodramatic reaction snaps me from my thoughts of Liam and I nudge her away from the box before bending to tear open the tape.

"Get a grip, it's not alive, nor is it some famous person's head."

"But it could be a non-famous person's head."

I stop pulling at the tape and look up to see if she's serious, typically for Laura-Nel, she is.

"Be of some use and grab me some scissors or a knife, this tape is noisy and I don't want to upset Seren."

She gives me a small salute, backing away towards the kitchen but never taking her eyes from the box in case something jumps out and bites her.

A few moments later, she's back with a sharp knife.

"I figure we can use it as a weapon if needs be."

I shake my head at her level of crazy and gently begin to cut through the tape.

When the box is finally open, I gingerly pull back the flaps; my heart rate escalates so much that it feels like a stampede of excited, Irish dancers are performing *River Dance* in my chest.

It has to be from Liam.

three

Stuck to the top of what looks like a canvas wrapped in more brown paper is a note.

Don't let sadness from the past or the fear of the future stop you from finding happiness in the present.
Today is not about old memories but about making new ones.

I gently pass the note to Laura-Nel to read and carefully begin to remove the brown paper.

The image revealed beneath, is one that causes my heart to expand, squeezing the oxygen from my lungs. It's so beautiful, I literally struggle to breathe through the emotions that flood me.

I stare at a vision of me holding Seren's hand while we walk alone through what can only be described as paradise.

Wildflowers grow at our feet in vibrant shades of life, trees open up to allow us safe passage, their leaves falling around us in a spectrum of colour and vivid butterflies dance at our arrival. It's the hand that appears from just out of focus, reaching out to hold mine that captures my attention, while Seren looks completely at peace, yet alert, happy and loved.

"Bloody hell!"

Laura-Nel's quiet exclamation and sudden appearance at my side makes me turn my head to look at her, but she's not looking at me, she's just as transfixed as I am on the image before us.

"That boy has mad skills," she says. Her words are filled with awe.

We both stand in silence, drinking in every inch. Our eyes are intoxicated with the colour and the life portrayed in front of us.

"What's in the other package?"

At her question, I look deeper into the large box and find a brightly wrapped gift with a big pink bow on the top.

When I don't move quickly enough to retrieve the second present, Laura-Nel takes that as her opportunity to grab it, turning over the tag attached and reading aloud the message, "For Seren – Happiness is blowing bubbles"

She looks to me for permission and I nod knowing I can't give Seren an un-screened present just in case it upsets her.

Ripping the paper off like it's Christmas, she reveals the gift within and exclaims, "Fuck me, who is this bloke and where can I get me one?"

In her hand is an expensive, children's bubble machine.

My already full to bursting heart swells even further at the most thoughtful gift that anyone has ever bought for my sister.

She loves bubbles.

How would he know she loves bubbles or is it just a lucky guess?

Either way, he still bought a gift for a child that he doesn't even know, just because she's mine.

three

I have to text him.

"You have to thank him."

I glance back at the beautiful artwork that leans up against the now empty box.

"I know."

Laura-Nel places the bubble machine on the floor by the coffee table and comes to stand next to me, wrapping her arm around my shoulder and following my gaze to the canvas before us.

"And by thank him, I mean with your body."

I snap my head to look at her, narrowing my eyes at her comment.

"What? It would be rude not to thank him for his kind and thoughtful gifts without at least some lip action."

"I'll text him."

She huffs, drops her arm and begins to collect the discarded wrapping paper.

"For once in your short but stubborn life, grab this opportunity by the balls and go and fight for your happiness. Don't let this chance pass you by; I have a feeling you will regret it more than you did the first time, so go and get your man and make him yours again."

"I…"

"Don't you dare tell me you can't or you're only letting him go because he deserves better; he wants *you* and you want *him*, the rest of life's shit is inconsequential."

I look at my friend in stunned silence before

finding my voice again. "I wasn't going to say that; I was going to say I'm ready to fight for him but your use of a word with five syllables kind of knocked me off course."

She shrugs casually, "It was on *Countdown* today. I've been waiting all afternoon for the opportunity to use it."

God, I love this girl.

"Well, smarty pants, I'm going to open one of those bottles, then you're going to help me find more words, with hopefully fewer syllables, to text to Liam."

She salutes me once more, "Supercalifragilisticexpialidocious." and then she heads straight for the kitchen.

"You know that's not a real word, right?" I call out to her.

I know she's taking a swig from the open bottle when a garbled, "Incontrovertible." is called from the kitchen.

I can't help but laugh.

God, I really do bloody love this girl.

chapter 18

Liam

Thank you is not enough. I am lost for words. I wish I could see you, then maybe I would feel less tongue-tied or maybe I would feel more. You are SO talented, Liam. I hope you continue to use your gift because the world would be a far less colourful place if you didn't. Seren will love her gift too; bubbles are one of her most favourite things. I miss you. I wish I could tell you in person how I feel about you but, for your sake, I should let you go. I can't though. I don't think I'll ever be able to let you go.

The text comes through at 2 am in the morning. I'd half given up hope of hearing from her, so when my phone vibrates, rousing me from my fitful sleep, my pulse spikes even before I open it.

She doesn't want to let me go.

She doesn't want to let me go and I refuse to lose her, so this might just be the best text I've ever received.

I reread the words at least a dozen times before my finger hovers above the keyboard to type out my reply.

Don't then. Don't let me go.

It takes her a few more minutes to respond, but instead of a text my phone rings with her incoming call.

"Hi."

This one, softly spoken word in her husky voice, completely melts away my fears.

She called me when she could have sent a text.

"Hi. I wasn't expecting you to call."

I can hear her hesitancy when she replies, "Oh, I'm…I didn't think. I know it's late, but when I got your text back so quickly I thought…I mean, I needed to hear your voice. I'm sorry. Maybe I can call back sometime tomorrow…if you want me to that is?"

I rush to allay her fears, the worry in her tone evident.

"No…No, I can talk now. I want to talk now, that's if you can?"

Her voice comes over the speaker like a warm breeze, "Yes, I can talk. As long as you don't mind me almost whispering. I…I can't risk waking Seren;

she seems to be having another good night's sleep and I can't afford to disturb her."

I smile and I'm hoping she can hear my relief, "I like it when you whisper."

I know she's smiling too because her voice, if possible, becomes even more gravelly, "You always did. I remember the nights when we would talk like this for hours. I always felt bad about keeping you up but not bad enough to stop. You got me through so many bad nights and you never even knew it."

"If I knew, I would have been there for you even more. You could have told me, Cari. I wish you had trusted me enough to tell me."

Her responding silence makes my breath catch and I'm afraid my words have closed the door on this conversation, "I…"

"No, please Liam, I have to speak…"

"Okay, I'm here, I'm listening."

"It wasn't about not trusting you, it was about not trusting myself. I felt like I was using you to finally be normal, to finally have something that was just for me. I wanted to keep you just for me."

She sighs lightly as though she's struggling to find the words, but continues, "Before everything, I was just Cari, just a girl with the world at my feet. Then…afterwards, that girl just disappeared; it was like I had been washed away on a raging torrent and I couldn't swim strong enough to find my way back. Until you; you made that girl come back. When I was with you I had the world at my feet again. For the few hours we would get to spend together every day, I would finally feel free. Then, I'd go back to my real life and get swallowed up again."

Her words are laced with guilt, but I don't want her to feel that way, "I'm happy I could be that for you, I want to be that for you again."

Her tired sigh sounds sad, "Don't you see, I was hooked on how you made me feel and on who I was when I was with you, but it wasn't real; it was a fantasy. I knew I was using you, I knew we couldn't go anywhere and yet I couldn't give you up."

Her admission just fuels me further, "Don't *you* see, I felt the same way about you. If I gave you freedom, it felt like you were giving me the entire world. If you were hooked on me, I was just as addicted to you. That's what love is, Cari. It's making someone's life better, just by being a part of it. It's giving someone the world, without even knowing you have. It's not selfish to want to keep ahold of that, especially when the other person feels the same way. It's right. It's so right, everything else feels wrong. Life is *wrong* without you and I refuse to keep feeling this way. There is nothing...*nothing*, standing between us. I hope you can see that now and if you can't I'm going to do everything within my power to convince you because love is also never giving up and when it comes to you I refuse to give up. So the question is, do you love me? Because I've just told you how much I love you."

I prepare myself to have to wait for her answer,

three

but she doesn't hesitate.

"I love you, Liam. I love you with all that I am and all that I have."

Her words are a balm to my broken soul.

"You don't know how long I've waited for you to say that. The time we've spent apart, it's fucking killed me."

"Liam..." she interrupts, but I'm not going to allow her to take back the words she just confessed.

"No, Cari. Don't you dare tell me, after all this, that we can't be together."

She actually lets out a small laugh and for a second I'm embarrassed by my forcefulness, "I wasn't, I was going to say I've missed you too. I've missed you so bloody much...but then you went all alpha-male on me and..." she drops her voice even further, "I have to say...it's kinda hot."

Her rasp works its way over my skin and settles in my groin.

I groan, half playfully, half with need, "You do realise I haven't had sex since..." she gasps and I halt my confession.

"Since when? What were you going to say?"

"It's nothing, you just have this effect on me, you drive me completely crazy."

Her voice is just a whisper, "You haven't been with anyone else since... us?"

Can I admit this to her? If I do, it's going to make me look so pathetic.

"There's only ever been you."

Shit. My mouth will not give me a break; I can't keep anything a secret from her.

On a deep, heavy exhale she replies, "Since us, there hasn't been anyone else for me either."

God. Does she know the effect those few words have on me?

They ignite all my nerve endings, bring goose bumps to my skin and stoke a desire so strong, it feels like electricity is skating down my spine and settling in my cock.

Within seconds, I am aroused almost to the point of pain and hearing her soft breaths directly into my ear only serves to exacerbate my situation.

"God, Cari. You can't say things like this to me when I'm unable to touch you. My fingers are fucking itching to touch you."

If possible, her breathing becomes even more pronounced and I take the opportunity to catch her unawares, not giving her time to deny me, "Can I see you tomorrow? I need to see you tomorrow."

The bubble that encases us pops; I can feel it with her sharp exhale, "I can't tomorrow. Seren is on summer break and only has playscheme three days a week."

My brain goes into overdrive; I'm not going to wait until next week to see Cari. "Let me take you both out. Does she like the zoo, or the park, or even the aquarium? We can even drive out to the seaside if you want. Just please, let me see you tomorrow."

I'm aware I may be begging, but all worries of

three

self-preservation go out of the window when it comes to her.

She hesitates for far too long, she's going to say no.

"Please, Cari. I'll take you both anywhere, just don't shut me out. I want to get to meet Seren properly, I want to become part of your life again, of both your lives. Say yes?"

Finally, and so quietly I almost miss it, she exhales the word, "Yes."

Relief floods me; she said yes.

I try and fail to dampen my obvious enthusiasm, "Great! What time shall I pick you both up? If you can decide now where you want to go, I'll pre-book the tickets so we don't have to queue. I don't know about Seren, but I hate queues."

A smile creeps into her voice when she replies, "She hates queues too."

"Great!.." I need to stop saying that, calm yourself down Li, "So, where to?"

"The aquarium would be perfect, it's Seren's favourite place."

"Great! I mean, that's…" I can't think of another word, my mind can only focus on getting to see her again, "wonderful…I'll pick you both up around 10.30 am? Do I need to get a car seat for Seren or does she already have one?"

She chuckles lightly, "We have one."

"Grea…umm, I mean awesome!" I'm so lame, "I'll let you get to sleep and I'll see you in the morning."

"Goodnight, Liam."

"Goodnight, Cari."

She hangs up after saying, "Sweet dreams."

Tomorrow is the day I finally get to chase my future.

Tomorrow is the day I make her mine again and this time, I won't ever let her push me away.

chapter 19

Cari

I'm nervously pacing the floor of my kitchen.

I gave up on trying to sit quietly in the living room with Seren over half an hour ago after noticing my ratcheted nerves were wearing thin and rubbing off on her.

So, in an attempt to calm myself, I made myself a cuppa, one that now sits cold on the countertop. Instead of calmly sitting down and drinking it, I pace and run my hands through my unruly hair.

It's 10.15 am and I know any second now, the doorbell will ring and I will be faced with the one person that I've never been able to fully curb my addiction to.

At 10.25 am the chime of the doorbell halts me in my tracks.

He's here.

He's here and I haven't been able to get my frantically beating heart under control.

Knowing I need to answer the door before he rings again and possibly upsets Seren, I propel myself down the hallway and peek out of the side window to see Liam mirroring some of my previous actions; his hand is nervously running through his wavy hair and he can't seem to keep still.

Getting visual confirmation that he is just as flustered as I am, instantly reassures me.

It lets me know I'm not in this alone and gives me the strength to open the door with a relaxed but confident smile.

"Hi, you're early."

His eyes drink in my features before he nervously looks over his shoulder, "I can wait in the car for a little while if you're not ready."

I instinctively reach out my hand to touch his arm, "No, no. Please, come in. I'm just not used to anyone being on time. My best friend, Laura-Nel, is always running late and if I'm honest, normally Seren and I are too."

I'm not sure if it's my touch or my words, but his face instantly relaxes and before I have a chance to step back, he's just a breath away from me; his lips hover over mine and his eyes search my face for permission.

Then, with a small intake of air, his mouth is on mine. The kiss is soft, sweet, gentle and yet passionate. His lips move over mine as though they are memorizing my taste before he slowly licks the seam and seeks entrance.

three

What starts out as a hesitant kiss hello, soon blooms into something more. Something so fierce, I feel my knees buckle and I have to lean into him to steady myself.

With his hand around my waist, he reluctantly breaks away and rests his forehead on mine.

"Wow! That was possibly the best hello I've ever had."

He blinks, his eyes moving down to my mouth then back up to search mine.

"We, ah…" he clears his throat softly, "We should really get going. I got tickets for entry at 11 am and I don't want Seren to have to cope with the bigger crowds."

If I hadn't already fallen for this man, his thoughtfulness and apparent understanding of my sister's needs would have sealed my fate.

"Let me just go and get her ready, if you want to set up her car seat it's stored in the cupboard under the stairs."

I give him these instructions, but I still haven't actually let him go. We are still joined at the head, hips and arms. My head has always been his, my arms have always yearned to hold him and my hips have always wanted that intimate connection I've only ever experienced with Liam.

My mind knows I need to let him go, but my entire body has other ideas.

Placing a soft kiss to the side of my mouth, then to my forehead, he releases me and takes a small step back.

"Okay, that sounds like a plan. You go and get Miss Seren ready and I'll set up the car."

After wrangling Seren into her jacket, grabbing her full rucksack of necessary supplies and ushering her out to the car, I finally remember to give her the photograph of the aquarium so she knows where we are going.

"Shall we see the fish?"

Her eyes never leave the photograph that she now grips tightly, but she does use her free hand to grab mine and tug me quite forcefully down the garden path.

I guess that's a yes.

Liam catches my eye as we approach and he smiles down at the little girl who is all but dragging me towards him.

"Someone seems eager. Shall we see the fish today Seren?" He bends down to her level but doesn't touch her or force her to acknowledge him, which warms my heart even more.

"Okay then, car first, then fish."

Without further prompting, Seren drags me towards the car, something I have never seen her do before.

It makes me laugh and I give Liam an appreciative smile.

"Seatbelt on. Let's go."

I strap Seren into her seat in the back of the car and I make sure she's settled. She's still holding the

three

photo that she hasn't yet taken her eyes off, so I make my way over to the passenger side and slip into the front seat.

"You're not like other people. You're so good with her. Do you have someone in your family with Autism?"

Liam starts the car and I watch as a faint blush rises over his cheeks.

"No, I've never met anyone with Autism before but I...I admit to doing some research over the last few days." He looks over at me shyly before continuing, "I just didn't want to do anything wrong."

I'm speechless.

He's spent the last few days researching ASD and all because he doesn't want to upset me or her.

All because he wants to understand, all because he accepts us, accepts her.

"I...I don't know what to say."

I can't take my eyes off him and watch as the blush on his cheeks deepens.

"You don't need to say anything. It's not a big deal."

"To me it is. To me, it's a *huge* deal. I...thank you."

He turns his gaze to me briefly, his dimple popping out when he smiles.

"I didn't just look on the internet. I... visited an expert, well as expert as anyone can be I guess. Please don't think bad of me when I tell you, but I visited

Seren's school."

"You what?"

He flicks his head sharply my way, before looking back at the road, one hand leaving the wheel to run through his hair.

"I didn't know it was Seren's school, I swear. I went there on behalf of my sister-in-law's foundation that helps local charities with fundraising and awareness. I went to offer our help and also to find out more about Autism. I promise, I didn't know it was Seren's school until I saw her there and I recognised her from the day we bumped into each other."

This is a lot to digest and the car descends into silence as he nervously waits for my judgment.

I still haven't spoken and around ten minutes later we pull up into the aquarium car park. On autopilot, I find Seren's blue, disabled parking badge in my bag and direct Liam into a yellow edged, disabled parking bay.

"I'm sorry, Cari. I didn't mean to overstep any boundaries."

He turns off the ignition and swivels in his seat to face me; before he has a chance to apologise again, my seat belt is off and I'm attacking his mouth with mine like a woman starved.

I swallow down his gasp of shock and dominate the kiss; my tongue forcing entry into his mouth, drinking him in like I need his very essence to survive.

three

The car begins to rock and moments later, after a few firm kicks to the back of my seat, I am wrenched out of my desire laced fog.

Seren is why the car is rocking; she is throwing herself back and forth in her seat, informing us she wants out of the car and into her favourite place. She knows exactly where we are and she's not happy about us not already being inside with her beloved fish.

He chuckles against my mouth and I give out a heavy sigh, "I think Miss Seren is ready to go." He pulls away from me, yet his eyes are still fixed on my kiss-swollen lips.

Seren's determination to leave the car increases and she lands a few swift kicks to the back of his seat, causing him to look towards my little sister who is now flapping her hands and rocking even more vigorously.

"You amaze me, Liam Fox."

His attention turns back to me and he stares at me like I'm the only woman in the whole wide world, "And you captivate me, Cari Pritchard."

An extra strong kick shakes my seat, snapping my attention back to Seren and our moment is over.

"Let's go see the fishies, Seren."

I get out of the car and open the back door to unbuckle her. As soon as the belt is free, she launches herself at me and lands a wet kiss right on my face.

"Soooos."

Oh. My. God.

She said it again and this time it was to me.

Tears immediately fill my eyes, but these are ones of overwhelming elation, not sorrow.

"Yes, sws."

I swallow down the powerful emotions that come from hearing my sister speak her first word and help her out of the car, resisting the urge to squeeze her tightly.

Watching the entire exchange, is Liam.

His face mirrors mine. Shock, awe and rapture all war for dominance, before his features settle on joy.

He gets it.

He gets why this moment is so special and in getting it, he steals yet another piece of my heart.

chapter 20

Liam

Today will go down as the *most perfect* day in the history of perfect days.

Watching Seren enjoy the aquarium, while holding Cari's hand, feels like I have finally come home; I am finally being allowed to be part of her life.

It is perfect in its simplicity.

Just being together, with no concerns about being caught, with no hiding away or having to worry what others may think of us, is totally freeing.

Anyone looking at us today would see a happy couple hand in hand, totally mesmerized by the little girl in front of us.

They would have no idea that I was once her student, or that she cast me aside with a mouthful of lies, albeit well-meaning ones.

They would just see us, Liam, Cari and Seren.

"Do you think she sees things differently than

us?" I nod towards Seren, who is happily hand-flapping away in front of a large fish tank and has been for the last twenty or so minutes.

"I mean, I just see water, some dull grey looking fish with big eyes and the occasional air-bubble."

We are sat on a small bench not three feet away from Seren, with our hands joined and Cari is leaning into my side, her head resting on my arm.

"I think the world we see is black and white, while Seren sees all the shades of the rainbow and more in-between. Where you see boring grey fish, she sees sparkling silver surrounded by movement; the ripple their fins make creating patterns that our mind doesn't grasp. Where you see plain water, she sees swirls of colour and the microscopic specks that dance around, suspended in perpetual motion; and where you see just one large bubble, Seren sees all the teeny tiny ones our eyes pay no attention to. They create a visual feast of movement across her senses. Combine all this together and she sees the complete spectrum, while we are left with the mundane."

"Wow, when you put it like that, I guess we are the ones missing out."

She looks wistfully over to her sister; pride and unconditional love pouring out of her for this special little girl.

"Those are just my guesses, but imagine seeing all that in *everything,* all the time, every, single, day. It's no wonder she gets overwhelmed. I think being able to see not only the big, obvious things, but all of the tiny things in-between, is both a blessing and a curse. That's without possibly hearing every noise in this place, from the motors of the fish tanks, to the buzzing of the electric lights overhead and then add on top of that all the smells and all the other people who surround her."

She drags her eyes away from her sister to look at me, "It may not be the most politically correct thing to say within the Autism community but if I could take her Autism away, I would. I would sell my soul to the devil to allow her to lead an independent life."

Her eyes flick back to the little girl filled with nothing but adoration, "Please do not think me selfish, I don't say that because of the strain it is to care for her, I say it because I want the world for her. I'd give her the whole world if I could, but to Seren, the world I want to give her can be a paralysing place."

We continue to watch her in silence. I'm not sure what to say to the picture Cari just painted of Seren's world.

Her following words are softly spoken but none less powerful.

"Yet for everything I've just said, I watch her on days like today, days when happiness for such a simple activity practically pours out of her and I know we can cope with the bad days; the days when I hate Autism more than I've ever hated anything in my life. The days when I curse Autism for taking away the sister I thought I had. The days when Autism causes her a pain that I cannot soothe away; the days when it prevents me from giving her comfort through the simple act of touch. The good days will always overcome the bad because she's Seren; because she is such a pure soul who lights up my otherwise dark life and has made me a better person. So although I wouldn't change her for the world, I will try my bloody hardest to change the world for Seren."

I lean away from her slightly in order to turn and face her. She sits up straighter and self-consciously pushes some loose strands of hair behind her ear, but doesn't turn to face me.

"Do you know what I see?"

I place my fingers on her chin and gently turn her face towards me. Her eyes hesitantly meet mine, "I see a little girl who is adored so much she wears that love like a protective suit. I think that suit of love shields her so well it allows her to have more good days than bad and allows her light to shine through."

I continue to hold her gaze even when I can see my words are making her eyes wet, tears threatening to spill over, "I see the person who has wrapped Seren in her protective suit, I see the sacrifices she has made to ensure that suit is as strong as it can be. I see that in protecting the person she loves more than anyone, she has abandoned her own needs and deserves someone to make sure she gets her own suit of love."

three

A single tear spills from her eye and runs lazily down the swell of her cheek. I use my thumb to carefully wipe it away, "Let me be the tailor of your own protection suit, I promise to make it as strong as I can, I promise to make sure it never slips off and I promise that it will not only wrap around you but Seren as well."

Her eyes close and she leans her face into my hand, my thumb is still lightly caressing her cheek, wiping away any further stray tears.

"I...I want to, Liam, so badly but..."

"There are no buts, there's nothing in this world that could make me want to be anywhere else. Every single molecule of my being, right down the marrow of my bones, knows this is where I'm supposed to be. You are my suit of love, I'm a better man when I'm with you."

She shakes her head slightly, her eyes opening to look into mine, "I hurt you so very badly, how can you ever forgive that?"

I can't help but smile, "Because in forgiving you I've healed myself; I know what you did wasn't meant to hurt me, I understand that completely, but not forgiving you, not being here with you, would just be a way to hurt myself more. Life is not meant for regrets; the past is the past for a reason and I want my future to be with you."

Her eyes close again and a light rush of air leaves her lips, "But what about your job? What about Ibiza?"

The fact she's giving thought to my job means she is finally accepting us being together, "I'll have to go back for a few weeks in order to give Nate a chance to replace me, but I've already got something else lined up."

My admission makes her eyes spring open, her lips form an oh shape before opening and closing a few times, "A job…or Uni?"

I toy with making her sweat a little, but decide I can't keep the information to myself, "A bit of both I guess."

I can see my vague answer just confuses her from the cute way her forehead scrunches up and her eyes squint a little, "I don't understand."

I can't help but kiss her, my lips haven't felt hers for far too long but I'm aware of the families around us so I just place a soft kiss on the corner of her mouth.

I glance over to check on Seren, even though the happy noises she's making inform me that she still hasn't moved from her spot at the fish tank I need to see she's okay, then I look back at Cari.

"I'm joining Isaac and we're opening a gallery together, well, actually he's opening a gallery and has promised me a section to display my work and…"

"And?"

"I've secured the funding for Seren's school and have volunteered to be their unpaid art teacher until I complete my Special Education Needs degree which I've already signed up for and will study on a part-time basis."

Whereas the little 'oh' her mouth formed a moment ago was cute, the gaping cavern her mouth forms now is downright hilarious and I try and fail to suppress a snort before I use my fingers to close her wide open jaw.

"If you stay like that you might catch flies."

She slams her mouth shut but looks no less shocked.

"You're not…I mean…it's not…"

"I'm not doing it for you, or for Seren or even to be noble. I'm doing this for me. I'm doing this because when I visited Seren's school it opened my eyes to something I never even considered before. This is my path."

We stare at each other for a long moment until Seren bounces over to us, unzips the bag that rests at Cari's feet and proceeds to pull out the contents.

Cari rushes to help her, "What do you want Seren? Drink? Crisps?"

Seren is now trying to force Cari's hand away so she can continue rifling through the bag.

"Damn, I forgot to bring her travel symbols so she can request things. I never forget them…I can't believe I forgot them."

I'm just about to offer to drive back and collect them when Seren pulls out a small container, pops off the lid and pulls out a biscuit. She then skips back over to the fish tank and begins to munch on her snack.

"I guess she's found what she wanted. Do you think it's time for us to go somewhere and have dinner if she's hungry?"

Cari grins and looks at me from the corner of her eye, "Are you going to be the one to move her on?"

I shrug and try to feign confidence, "It can't be that difficult surely?"

She has a wicked smile on her face when she replies, "Have at it, big boy."

"Do you have one of those traffic light timers like they have in school?"

Her head spins so fast in my direction, I worry she might get whiplash.

"How long were you at her school?"

"A few hours, why?"

"No, we don't have a timer…well, we do, but we use it at home, I've never thought to bring it out with us."

"Why did you ask me about the length of my visit?"

She begins to pack the items that Seren discarded back into the bag.

"Because you seem to know more about day to day Autism strategies than I did in the first few years of caring for Seren. I'm both shocked and impressed."

I bend to help her get everything collected and packed away, "Nah, I just saw her carer use one of those timers when she was in the sensory room with

three

Seren. Trust me, I'm utterly clueless, but I do have an idea if you'll let me try it?"

"Like I said, this is the toughest part of the day so if you can make it easier, I'm all for it, but if you make it worse, I won't kiss you for the rest of the day."

I catch her wicked smile as she zips the bag closed, "Isn't that punishing you as much as me? No pressure then I guess."

Before I can talk myself out of it, I walk over to Seren and pull out my phone, initiating the timer app I use when I go to the gym.

You can set the length of the timer and it has a visual feature to show you the time counting down. It's a large circle, kind of like a pie and it slowly fills up with red until the pie, or whatever you want to call it, is full.

I think back to the words her carer used in the sensory room, set the timer to five minutes and crouch down next to Seren who pays me no attention.

Laying the phone flat against the glass of the tank, I hit the timer to begin and say "Seren, five minutes until fish are finished."

It's only brief, but I catch her eyes flick from the screen of my phone and then back to the fish.

When the first minute passes, I repeat the countdown, "Seren, four minutes until fish are finished," and again her eyes glance at the timer on my screen.

I repeat this countdown at each minute and when the time fills up I say, "Seren, fish finished."

What happens next nearly knocks me flat on my arse.

Without hesitating Seren turns to me, repeats the sound she made earlier in the car park that sounds like "sooooos" and lands me with a wet smacker right on my lips.

Then, without waiting, she grabs my hand and leads me away from the fish tank forcing Cari to scramble to catch up with us.

"Bloody hell, what are you? Are you like some kind of horse whisperer but for kids?"

I don't bother to hide the utter disbelief from my face, "I don't know about that, but what I do know is you owe me so much more than a few kisses."

chapter 21

Cari

Lips.

Skin.
Breath.
Touch.
Heat.
So much heat, I fear my clothes may spontaneously catch fire and turn to ash.

What started jokingly as Liam collecting his payment for his astounding 'Seren wrangling' skills, soon escalates.

After putting Seren to bed no more than thirty minutes ago, we lie stretched out on my sofa, our late dinner of fish and chips from the local chippie, all but forgotten.

"God, Cari, you feel so good."

His words end on a groan when I nip my teeth across his jaw, down to the base of his neck. His hips grind against mine, stoking the heat in my veins to dangerous levels.

"I want you. I want you so much."

I'm not ashamed of the need that laces my words. I want him more than I've ever wanted anything before.

"Let me take you to bed."

He pulls away from my hungry mouth, his hips unable to fully stop their movement but he tries his best to cool things off, "I...I wanted to take this slowly with you. I wanted to make sure this is what you truly want. I swear I can't do this again with you if you're not all in."

I brazenly lift my hips, searching out even more of him.

"I want this. I want you. I'm not going anywhere and I'm sorry you will always now think that I am. I promise to show you, in every way I can, that I want to be all in with you."

I'm a wanton, needy and panting mess.

I need this connection with him; I need him to show me he forgives me and I crave the feeling of us becoming one again.

He stills completely, the intensity of his gaze fueling the fire that rages deep inside me and setting my nerves on edge.

If he pulls away now I will be mortified. I don't think I could face that level of rejection especially

three

after the day we've just spent together; a day where he has, if possible, embedded himself even deeper into my heart and soul.

His mouth opens as if he's about to speak but then closes just as quickly. In one, swift movement, I am scooped up into his arms, my legs instinctively wrapping around his waist and he wastes no time in striding towards the stairs.

He takes the steps carefully, his arms tightening their hold on my thighs and his head leans down to whisper in my ear, "You asked for this, Cari. You asked for all of me; you told me you're all in."

"I am." The words escape me on a shiver.

He leans even closer so his lips now brush the shell of my ear, his whispers ghosting over the sensitive skin, "Make sure to be as quiet as possible when I finally take what you've just promised me. I'm not going to hold back, I'm incapable of doing so because I've waited for this…waited for you, for far too long."

I swallow down the moan that tries to escape after hearing his sensual threat.

He stops at the top of the stairs in a silent question of where I want him to take me. Liam's never been in my bedroom before, in fact, no man ever has. I nod my head towards the door at the end of the landing, past Seren's bedroom and the main bathroom.

When we reach the threshold he slowly allows me to slide down his firm body, until my toes reach the floor.

I can feel every, solid, muscle and another shiver threatens to roll over me.

Eyes locked on mine, he twists the door handle and leads me inside, flicking on the light switch as he goes.

My room is illuminated in bright white light and I rush to turn on the bedside lamp. When I turn the main light off and face him, his eyes are no longer on me but on the artwork that spans my walls.

His gaze skims over portraits of my Mum and Dad, then Seren as a baby; even Laura-Nel is immortalised and has a place on my wall. His eyes eventually rest on the final piece I have displayed and I let him drink in every brush stroke.

It's an oil painting of us; one created out of a perfect memory.

It's uncanny how this picture of just the two of us is so similar to the last gift he sent me.

We lie in a field of wildflowers, my head on his bare chest, my wild hair fanned out around us. One of his hands runs through the strands while the other holds my thigh hooked over his.

He stares at the sky lost in his own thoughts and I have my eyes closed, a look of complete peace on my face.

This was one of the few days we spent together outside of the allotment garden. I convinced him to come with me on a scouting trip for some inspiration and we spent the day in the countryside, wading

three

through cool streams, eating a picnic lunch under a large oak tree and making love in a meadow.

It was reckless of us considering the nature of our relationship but it was close to his exams and I knew that one way or another, I would be forced to give him up soon.

"I lost my boxers that day. I secretly told myself you kept them because you wanted to sniff them later." He looks over his shoulder at me giving me a wicked smile.

"Who said I didn't?" I deadpan.

His eyes flare for a second and then he laughs quietly, ever mindful of my sister only being two rooms down.

"I think I just lost them in the rush to get dressed when we heard those voices coming our way."

"I'll never tell, so you're always going to wonder if they now sit under my pillow or got eaten by a hungry bull."

His eyes twinkle with humour, "I rather like the thought of them still being under your pillow."

I flick my eyes to the bed and I can see the moment the light bulb goes off over his head. We both leap for it at the same time but with longer legs and more power, Liam gets there before me and flips over my pillows before I can even climb over his back.

"Aha! My lucky pants!"

He rolls over underneath me waving the boxers

out of my reach.

"Give them back! Finders keepers, losers weepers."

He chuckles, the action causing me to bounce around on his well-defined chest as I try and fail to grasp the evidence of my stalker tendencies.

"I hope you washed these, Cari. It would be pretty unhygienic to have my tighty whities under your pillow, unwashed for almost 2 years."

"Give. Them. Back."

"No, no. Like you said, finder's keepers and all that…unless…" the glint in his eyes gets even more mischievous, "unless you want to model them for me."

"Liam…" my voice tries and fails to come out as a warning. The thought of wearing them and nothing else reignites the heat inside me.

"Fair's fair, Cari. Maybe if you model them for me now, I'll let you keep them forever this time and forfeit the right to tease you about stealing them."

I don't hesitate, "Deal." His shock at my easy capitulation gives me the upper hand and I snatch back the undies before he has time to react.

"Hey, don't go backing out on our deal. You just agreed to wear them for me."

Shoving the undies, (clean I might add because of course I washed them, I'm not that depraved) on top of my head like some bizarre chef's hat/beret. I giggle uncontrollably at my cleverness.

I don't get to giggle for long as faster than I can

blink, I am picked up, dropped on the bed and fully beneath the manly, hard body I can't wait to unwrap.

"I've missed this; missed being silly with you, missed laughing with you."

The sincerity in his eyes almost brings back my guilt until his lips once again meet mine and his hands, with those talented artist's fingers, begin to skim over my body, relearning every inch and crevice.

When his hands reach the button of my jeans he breaks our kiss, checking my face for any sign that I want him to stop. My answer is to lean up slightly and pull my *Catfish and the Bottlemen* band t-shirt over my head, exposing my basic, black cotton bra.

His fingers fumble when he catches sight of my exposed skin, but he quickly refocuses and pops open the top button. His fingers fumble once more on the zip as I reach around my back and unsnap the clasp of my bra, allowing the straps to fall down my arms and my small breasts to bare themselves to his greedy gaze.

He finishes working the zip but doesn't immediately pull down my jeans, instead he leans forward and gently licks around my belly button, gaining a full body shiver from me. Then his warm, gentle mouth works it's way northwards, carving a path between my breasts, up over my collarbone and behind my ear.

"You can keep my undies, on the condition I get to keep yours."

My incoherent reply is due to his sensual tongue

licking my left nipple while his nimble fingers slowly circle the other.

His mouth pays such gentle attention, to each in equal measure, I all but yell at him to move his ministrations elsewhere.

"More, I need more." I pant out as my hips undulate against his strong thigh, seeking relief.

"Hush, patience is a virtue," he whispers between licks of his talented tongue and sucks of his equally talented mouth.

"I've waited so long, so long, Cari, that I am going to take my time. You promised me you're all in, so that means you're mine to savour."

After a particularly exquisite pull from his mouth he continues, "Besides, once I get inside you I'm afraid I won't be able to stop. I need to make you see stars long before I sink into you for the first time because when I do, it's going to be hard and fast. I will be too far gone to hold back, so let me worship you."

He blows lightly on my swollen peaks, causing them to tighten even further and then languorously makes his way, with open mouthed wet kisses, down to the apex of my thighs.

Using his shoulders to open my legs further, he gently bites through my jeans directly on to my most sensitive area causing me to gasp loudly and my hips lift involuntarily.

The thick fabric might have taken the edge off the bite, but the positioning couldn't have been more

three

perfect, sending zings of electricity right to my long neglected clitoris; one touch of his mouth through two layers of clothing almost made me come undone.

He looks up at me from between my spread thighs, his index finger now firmly tracing the seam of my jeans, "Shall I take these off now, Cari?"

"God. Yes." I all but growl, not bothered by how completely needy I am to have those firm lips and that talented tongue devouring me without any barriers.

My jeans are off before I can blink, my knickers soon follow and then he's there, nipping at the sensitive part of my inner thigh before connecting his eyes with mine and lazily licking up my core in one broad stroke.

I am unable to maintain eye contact as my head drops back and my eyes close of their own accord; my hands fisting in his hair as I beg him not to stop. He takes heed of my pleading and puts his mouth on me in a relentless assault, causing me to lose purchase on his hair and grip the bed sheets instead. My undoing is when he uses his fingers in tandem with his rhythmic licking and sucking. I fly apart in a shower of electricity and heat, the shout that escapes my lips is loud enough to wake the dead, but in this moment I have no thought of waking Seren or of anything really. I can only feel him.

He continues to lap at me until I come down from the ceiling and only stops when I beg him, stating I can't take any more.

I am completely boneless and only vaguely aware of him stripping off his clothes and then sheathing his cock with a condom. He crawls up the bed towards me and runs the tip of his hard-on through my arousal, my slick flesh eagerly wanting more even though I've just had one mind-blowing orgasm.

"Look at me, Cari. Please."

I fight to come down from my high and open my eyes, feeling him smiling against my breasts, that wicked tongue mimicking the light thrusts of his hips.

"Look at me, I need you to see me when I finally make you mine again."

My eyes connect with his and we both still, our breaths halting until that moment when he pushes fully inside.

A look of agonizing ecstasy takes over his face and then no more words are spoken.

We are just lips.

Skin.

Breath.

Touch.

Heat.

So much heat, we become seared onto each other's souls.

chapter 22

Liam

I wake alone in Cari's bed.

When we'd fallen asleep last night our limbs entwined after relearning every inch of each other's skin, I thought we'd wake up the same way.

Instead, I'm alone, the side of the bed Cari slept on, long gone cold.

I scan my eyes around her room, my gaze falling once more on her art-adorned walls.

This time, instead of staring at the image of us both in the meadow, I am drawn towards the image of her parents.

Both sisters take after their mother; they both have her emerald eyes and porcelain skin, but whereas Cari also shares her mother's wild auburn hair, Seren, has the same glossy, dark locks of their father.

It's the look her parents share, captured forever on canvas, that etches itself on my memory; a look of pure adoration and love.

I see the same look on my own parent's faces whenever they are in the same room and it is evident that Cari's parents shared the same type of relationship; one built on a solid foundation of love.

For a moment, I wonder what life would be like if I lost both my parents so young and a pang of hurt sears my chest.

If I've felt empty the last few years without Cari, I can only guess at the level of isolation and loneliness she has felt losing half her family in quick succession.

We talked last night for hours, her head on my bare chest, our legs tangled and my hand drawing soothing circles on her back. We shared our history with complete honesty.

I told her about travelling the world, about meeting Emma and about her marrying Jake. She told me about her art classes, her best friend Laura-Nel and her ambition to take a full-time position as an art teacher instead of the two part-time roles she has now.

We were just Cari and Liam sharing our lives; not a teacher and her student, hiding away from the world in fear of the repercussions.

It was exactly what I'd always dreamt it would be.

Perfect.

Noise from downstairs gets my attention and I quickly pull on my clothes, but not before I tuck the

three

black boxers I wore last night underneath her pillow with the other pair she originally stole from me.

It makes me grin to myself and I remember exactly how much fun we always had together as we both share the same weird sense of humour.

The noise from downstairs gets significantly louder, so I head that way wishing I could brush my teeth to rid me of my morning breath.

As I approach the living room, I hear the noises get more pronounced and an almighty crash, that sounds like a piece of furniture being tipped over forces me into a jog.

The scene that greets me is one I could never have expected.

The coffee table has been tipped over, Seren's puzzles haphazardly strewn all over the floor and Cari is crouched down at the side of the table, cleaning what looks like vomit from the hardwood floor. Seren is lying on the rug on the opposite side of the room, frantically thrashing and kicking her feet as hard as she can against the frame of the sofa.

Her noises are so loud and distressing that Cari hasn't even heard me enter and I'm not really sure what to do to help them both; this is way beyond my limited and newly founded 'Seren Wrangling' skills, which are more luck than judgment.

I don't even know what the cause of Seren's obvious meltdown is.

I carefully walk towards the upended coffee table to help tidy up and the movement catches Cari's eye.

She turns towards me slightly and I can see a small gash above her right eyebrow, her face a mask of pain she attempts to hide behind a shaky smile.

I immediately rush to her side, "What the hell happened?"

She averts her gaze and continues to clean the mess at her feet, which is indeed vomit.

I take the cleaning product and cloth from her hands and turn her face to look at me.

Her eyes fill with tears and her voice wobbles when she replies, "I forgot to plug in Seren's iPad, she always has it after breakfast but when I went to get it for her, it was dead. I didn't put it on charge last night."

Her admission washes over me and I know that it didn't get charged because of me; I have caused the distress this little girl is experiencing this morning. Guilt fills my stomach with bile and I gently run my thumb over her brow, just below the cut that thankfully isn't bleeding much.

"How did this happen?"

"She didn't understand, when she got her iPad, why it wouldn't work and at the time, I didn't realise it was out of power, so I gave it to her when she requested it and then went into the kitchen to tidy up. I heard her getting increasingly upset and walked back in just as she threw the iPad across the room. I didn't understand why she would do that so I shouted at her and made everything worse. She then got so upset she vomited, so I tried to distract her

three

with her puzzles to give me a chance to clean up, but puzzle time comes after iPad time and she got so frustrated she lifted the whole table and flipped it over. I was bending down cleaning up at the time and the edge caught me and caused that," she motions to the gash I'm still staring at, "She...she didn't mean to do it and I can't seem to get her to calm down. If she continues she'll vomit again and might even start biting herself but I just...I just don't know what to do."

Her eyes close on a small sob and the tears that filled her eyes now spill over.

I look towards Seren, still thrashing and kicking out and know I have to try and fix this.

"What does she like to do on the iPad?"

Cari shakes her head, her eyes still closed, more tears overflowing, "It doesn't matter, it doesn't have enough charge yet, it'll be at least an hour before she can have it."

"Just trust me, please? What does she like to do on it?"

"She likes...a mandala app and umm...she likes to watch her favourite show on *Youtube*."

I stand and pull out my iPhone from my back pocket, quickly searching for the right app and hitting install.

"What programme does she watch?"

Cari looks up at me and sees what I'm doing, "You...you can't give her that, she might break it."

"If she does, I'll buy another. Now, what

programme does she watch?"

She looks unsure as she tells me the name of a popular kid's TV show and I load it into *Youtube*. Once I have both of her favourite things set up, I walk quietly over to Seren, stopping a few inches from her side.

She is completely oblivious to my presence, her little body caught up in the throws of a violent meltdown and I worry she will end up hurting herself.

I turn the volume up to full blast and press play; the theme tune of her favourite show fills the air over the noise of her distress.

It takes a few moments, but I can see her slowly calm; her movements and cries become more subdued until she turns her head towards the sound and sees the small screen I have turned to face her.

Her little hands snatch away my phone between one blink and another and her meltdown stops, seemingly as quickly as it started. The only noise in the room now is the song she keeps playing over and over again on repeat.

Soft arms wrap around my waist from behind and I can feel the sobs from her chest through my back.

"Hush, we've sorted it. She's happy now."

I turn and gather a tearful Cari into my arms.

Her sobs turn to hiccups and she half cries, half chuckles, "The child whisperer strikes again."

We stand, just holding each other amongst the noise of a too loud children's show song, vomit still

three

on the floor, an overturned table and puzzles strewn everywhere, but despite it all, this feels right.

Just over an hour later, I kiss Cari goodbye on her doorstep and physically force myself out of her arms.

She's got an art class tonight so I've arranged to pick her and Seren up tomorrow for a day at the beach.

When I arrive back home, I enter the kitchen to a cacophony of noise.

Sat around the central island are H, Isaac and both my parents.

The noise is due to H telling them about his latest dating disaster and his hook-ups over friendly pussy and by pussy, I'm assuming he means a cat. Well, I'm hoping it's a feline or else talking about it in front of my folks is a whole other level of inappropriateness.

"So the bloody thing wails like it's about to die and then pounces on my Davidson like it's a freaking mouse it wants for its dinner. I only just manage to save my crown jewels from its three inch, sharp as fuck, killer claws," he begins to pull down the zipper of his fly and drags his jeans over his hips.

"Oh, God, Harry, put your meat and two veg away, I don't want to be seeing it," my mother laughs covering her eyes.

"I'm not showing you the goods, Mrs. F, I'm

showing you my battle scars," and with that he pulls the denim further down his thigh and reveals deep claws marks gouged into his skin.

"Look at what the little tabby bastard did to me! Then do you know what she said?...." he looks at us, pausing for effect, "She said 'I think it's time for you to leave, you've upset Mr. Puss Puss.'..." he looks around at us in comedic disbelief, "...I've upset Mr. Fucking Puss Puss!... I'm telling you, that girl was crazy in the coconuts and me and my Davidson were lucky to make it out alive. I grabbed my stuff and legged it out into the street in just my *Calvin Klein's*. I'm just glad it was gone midnight because me and Davidson were both totally deflated by now and we didn't want the stress of an audience. I think I'm scarred for life."

Isaac, who is trying to hold in his laughter and be serious asks, "Why do you call your dick, Davidson?"

H gives him a look as if to say 'Duh' then clarifies, "Harry David Brown, therefore my pecker is Harry-David's-son... Davidson. Pretty self-explanatory I think and not the question I was expecting after just telling you I was viciously attacked by some crazy bird's pussy last night!"

His voice is filled with righteous indignation and only serves to make us all snicker. I full on snort when my father asks, "And what number was last night's bird then H? Nine? Ten?"

He begins to answer as he readjusts his jeans and zips them back up, "She was number twelve."

three

I'm not sure of the significance of the numbers so I ask from my spot propped up in the doorway, "Number twelve?"

All heads turn to me, now only realising that I've witnessed the whole retelling of 'Pussy-gate'.

Isaac enlightens me, "Number twelve, post-balls."

I'm still confused, "Post-balls?"

With a resigned sigh H plonks himself down on a stool and puts his head in his hands, his voice is muffled when he speaks, "The twelfth girl I've hooked up with since I had my nadgers removed."

My mother motions me to tread carefully on the subject by widening her eyes and nodding her head towards H, but I can't let the opportunity pass; I know H certainly wouldn't, had our roles been reversed.

"So, if things with number twelve went so well, I can't wait to find out what happens with unlucky, for some, thirteen."

I walk towards the spare stool and sit next to Isaac, who holds his hand up for a high-five.

"Nah, Li-Li, H is gonna turn this around and number thirteen will blow his mind. Ain't that right, H? You can't keep a good man down."

I'm afraid to ask, but can't help myself, "What happened to the other post-ball, hook-ups numbers one through eleven?"

A chorus of, "Don't ask!", comes from everyone in the room, including a still downcast, H.

"Okay, Okay, I'm not asking! I just think you need to channel your inner *Dirk Diggler*."

H pops his head up to look at me, "*Dirk Diggler?*"

I nod and pour myself a juice from the jug in front of me, "Yeah, you know, the porn star in the film *Boogie Nights*. He made thirteen work for him, so you can make it work for you. It doesn't have to be an unlucky number."

Everyone looks at me like they haven't got a clue what I'm talking about until my mother breaks the silence, "I'm not sure a thirteen-inch member can ever be unlucky darling."

"Mother!" Isaac groans, "How the hell do you know how long his member was?"

She smiles innocently, looking over to my father before looking back at us, "I'm not ancient just because I'm your mother, I watched that film with your father. Very entertaining it was too."

While myself and Isaac both shake our heads, H pipes up, "Your mother is seriously cool. She watches Hollywood porn and knows the size of the leading character's Davidson."

This conversation is heading in a seriously weird direction, so I change the subject quickly, "I'm going to see Nate later, before he heads off with Liv. They are off to catch up with Jake and Emma in The Seychelles."

"That's nice, son. Say Hi to him and tell him a phone call home to his mother more often, wouldn't

three

go amiss."

"I will, but that's not why I'm telling you. I'm handing in my notice and coming back for good."

That gets everyone's attention and my mother springs up from her seat, rushing over to me and squeezing me in one of her death grip hugs.

"You're really coming home? I'm so happy! Are you signing up for University? What's with the change of heart? Oh, I know, it's a girl isn't it?"

Dad comes over and pats me on the back, effectively saving me from death by squeezing and from all of the questions she's just launched at me.

"I do have a plan," I say, once she's let me go, "I just have to finalise all the details and once everything is in place, I'll fill you in, I promise."

"Congrats on the life-changing decision buddy." H calls out from over the counter, "I'm happy for you, man."

"Cheers, H."

Isaac also gives his approval by coming over and ruffling my hair, "Can't wait to find out all the juicy details. Just don't let Nate give you any grief about quitting, you know how he gets about his clubs."

"I won't, Iz, besides, I'll offer to go over until he finds someone to replace me. I have to empty my apartment and get all my stuff but I should only be gone for a week or two max."

"Can't wait to have you back home, son," my father replies, guiding my mother into his arms.

This is the perfect time to drop the second and

infinitely bigger bomb.

"I'm not going to be coming back home, I'm going to look for my own place."

Silence, followed by my mother's strained voice a good sixty seconds later, "But why on earth do you need to move out when we have more than enough room for you here? If it's good enough for Isaac to stay at home…"

I interrupt her quickly wanting to shut down the inquisition, "I've lived on my own for a long time now, Mum. I really enjoy having my own space."

She goes to say more but good old Dad saves my bacon again, "He's right, it's good for a man to find his own way," then after a worried glance at Isaac adds, "Not that it's not good for you to stay home either, Iz. I just mean I support your decisions no matter what you choose."

He holds my mother a little tighter, sensing her need to grill me about my choice.

"Thanks, Dad. It means a lot, in fact, I was wondering if you and Mum could help me by checking out some flats while I'm gone, so I have a good selection to view when I get back? What do you say, Mum, up for the task of finding me somewhere suitable to rent?"

The smile on her face is forced, "Of course I can. I'll contact a few estate agents later today."

I walk over and place a kiss on her cheek, "Thanks, Mum. You're the best, you know that?"

Her smile in response is small but more genuine,

three

"I just worry about you that's all. All my boys are leaving me and I find it hard to let go, but you know I support you. Just give me a day or two to digest it all and then I'll find you the best bachelor pad ever."

I kiss her again, give my goodbyes and head up to my room to call Nate.

Thirty minutes later, after another inquisition from Nate, it's agreed I'll go back to Ibiza for ten days to hand over the reigns to Rhian and pack up all my stuff to be shipped home.

Throughout all the questions thrown at me by everyone, I've managed to keep what's going on between Cari and I quiet for now. What we have is still so delicate and new, that I want to keep her to myself for a while longer before exposing her to the Fox-Williams clan in all its splendor. Plus, we still have things to discuss.

I know she wants to be with me and I want to be with her, but there are still a few hurdles to overcome.

I'm not worried, though; I know what we have is greater than any obstacle that can be placed in our path.

chapter 23

Cari

Liam has been gone for two days and I feel his absence deeply.

Over the last week we've spent every spare moment together and riding the high of that bliss, made it easier to crash and burn when he left.

"He's coming back, Cari," Laura-Nel says between sips from her wine glass.

"I know that. I'm just adjusting that's all. After a week of the sweetest sugar rush, I'm just having withdrawals I guess."

"Will I finally get to meet him when he comes back? I promise to be on my best behaviour and not to say anything too mortifying." She waggles her eyebrows meaning she can't wait to spill everything about me.

"You couldn't bloody button it if your life depended on it. Don't worry, I've already warned him you're a terrible over-exaggerator."

three

I try and fail to smother my smile by taking a sip from my own glass.

"Pah. The boy needs educating. He should feel indebted to me for providing him with juicy, never before heard of gossip about the woman he's in love with."

I cock a brow at her, "First off, please stop calling him 'boy' and secondly, lay off the love talk. We've only said it to each other once when we initially got back together and I'm not sure we are ready to be constantly throwing a word like that around willy-nilly."

She cocks her own brow in a mocking gesture, "Purleease, that boy has loved you since he was seventeen and you feel the same way. It's time for you to admit it and do so frequently. In fact, I think given your history, you should be the first one to say it again. When he comes back you need to tell him you're crazy about him."

"Again, you used the term boy. Trust me, he's all man."

"Stop trying to divert me with hints of his sexual prowess. I'm being serious here, Cari. You need to be the one to make the first move and you know it."

I look at her with wide eyes, "Wow! I never thought I'd see the day that I'd get chastised by you. Who are you and what have you done with my friend?"

She smiles mischievously and speaks around the rim of her glass, "Oh, she's still in here and still wants all the deets of your action between the sheets."

I roll my eyes and reach for the bottle to refill my glass, "Since when have I ever given you deets?"

"A girl always has to try, besides you get more loose-lipped the more vino you sink, so bottoms up!" she gulps down the last of her wine and grabs the bottle, shaking it in the hopes of finding more than just the dregs that remain.

"We're out. Please tell me you have more."

I shake my head and offer her what's left of my glass.

"No, you need that more than me and since we've finished off both bottles, I think it's time for me to get some shut eye on your couch just in case the little madam makes an early entrance."

"You don't have to stay tonight, I'm not too tired this week as Liam shared my Seren duties before he left and I've had more sleep than ever before."

"Like I said, that boy…" she notices my stern gaze, "…I mean that *man* is one of a kind. You need to lock that one down and never let him go."

"Thanks for your wise words, oh great one, now are you staying or going because this stuff has gone to my head and I think I need to sleep it off while I can."

She gets up from her place on the floor where she's been sat cross-legged for the last few hours and groans as she stretches out her legs.

"If you don't need me, I think I'll head off, I've got an extra shift tomorrow so the sleep will go to

three

good use… but only if you're sure. I know this is the only evening you get to recharge your batteries."

I stand and stretch, then walk towards her to wrap her in a tight hug, "I'm sure, let me go call you a cab."

"I love you, Cari."

"I love you, Laura-Nel."

She lets out a small laugh, "See, it's easy to say, isn't it? So make sure to say it to your b… I mean *man* soon. He deserves to hear it too."

"Yes, okay, you're right, oh wise and wonderful relationship guru. Remind me to give you just as much grief when you finally decide on just one guy instead of the scores you discard without thought."

"Hah! I think you'll find I give them all plenty of thought, you just ain't gonna wanna know what my thoughts are…"

"You're right… I don't. Now get going before I change my mind and make you stay."

Seren unusually sleeps well and I actually feel like a semi-alive person the following day, despite my small hangover.

She's back in summer school today and I have no classes, so once I've dropped her off I have some rare free time.

I should use it as an opportunity to catch up on laundry and housework, but instead, I head to the high street to indulge in some window shopping.

I'm browsing through my favourite arts and crafts store, when my phone vibrates and I eagerly dig through my bag to find it, all the while hoping it's Liam.

He's been so busy in Ibiza, I've told him not to worry about contacting me; I just want him to do what he has to do as quickly as possible and then hurry back to me.

I miss my lucky boxers

His cheeky text makes me snort out loud and I quickly scan the store to see if anyone is watching me.

No one is paying me any attention so I send back a quick reply.

I'm keeping them safe. In fact, they are very comfortable on under my jeans

With my eyes on my phone, I'm not really paying attention to my surroundings and walk smack-bang into another person.

"I'm so sorry, I wasn't looking where I was going."

The lady I've ploughed into picks up the item she's dropped and stands to look at me, "It's okay, dear, I..." recognition hits her face when she finally looks up at me and she breaks out a smile that is so reminiscent of her son's. "Miss Pritchard, it's so

three

lovely to see you. It must be two years since Liam's end of year art show. I hope you are well, you look great."

I splutter, looking for a reply, but the cat has firmly got my tongue, or in this case, Mrs. Fox-Williams has.

"Are you still teaching at the college?" she doesn't wait for a reply, "Liam is coming home soon; I'll make sure to tell him I bumped into you, I'm sure he would love to catch up and maybe visit the college again."

I force a smile; I am incapable of speech and Mrs. Fox-Williams takes this as her cue to keep talking.

"We were so proud of him for winning the end of year show. His piece was truly magnificent and now adorns our living room wall. You brought out the best in him and really allowed his talents to shine. Thank you so much for all your hard work with him."

I manage to squeak out, "Liam didn't need my help, his talent is so great that all I did was give him subjects to paint and then admire whatever he produced. He's very gifted, Mrs. Fox-Williams."

My praise for her son makes her beam with pride and I currently feel like the biggest fraud on the planet.

What am I to say?

That the only talent I helped him develop was far more lascivious than different art techniques.

Instead I settle for, "Well, it was lovely to see

you." To which I get a cheery, "You too, my dear. Take care." And then I make a hasty exit, almost forgetting to put the pack of pens in my hand back on the shelf; the last thing I need right now is to get done for shoplifting.

I hurry away as fast as I can from the little store and slip into a small café, hoping to sit at the back and calm my nerves.

I order a large cup of tea and take it to the very back table, as far away from the front windows as possible, just in case she sees me again.

My hands shake as I take my phone from my pocket and text the only person who will know exactly how I'm feeling right now.

I just bumped into your mother. Literally. She remembers me from your art show. I feel sick.

I set the phone down on the table and take a large sip of my steaming, hot brew. It burns slightly on the way down, but I don't care, I need to replace the bile in my belly with warmth before I vomit; I guess that's a trait I share with Seren after all.

When it buzzes across the tabletop, I swipe the screen, all the while wishing he wasn't so far away.

How could anyone forget u? You're beautiful. Please don't stress about this. We can talk when I get home about how u want

three

2 tell my parents about us. If u want me 2 lie 2 them, I won't like doing it, but for u I will. So u think about what would make u more comfortable and I'll do all I can 2 make it easier for u. I miss u.

I want to tell him that I love him so much and miss him too, but I settle on a cowardly reply instead, not wanting to lay my heart on the line more than I already have.

I miss u soooo much

His reply is instant.

Not long baby, I'll be home in just a few days. Can't wait 2 see my girls

This man owns me.
He misses me, misses us.
His text steals yet another piece of my heart and soul.

chapter 24

Liam

The last ten days have dragged, despite me being so busy that I've only managed a few texts to Cari and a handful of phone calls.

Nate flew over on my last day, just to oversee everything and, I think, to check I didn't want to change my mind.

Nothing and no one could possibly change my mind.

"I'm hoping this isn't a rash decision because of a woman, little bro," he asks on our way to the airport where he's offered to drive me.

I give him a look that brokers no argument, "My choices are mine alone, but in answer to your nosiness, no, my decision isn't based entirely on a woman, although I have met someone…well, when I say met someone, I mean reconnected with someone."

He looks like he wants to ask more, but unlike

three

my other brothers, Nate isn't one to overly pry, believing everyone has the right to make or break their own life however they wish.

I not so subtly change the subject, "So, how's things going with Liv? I thought with Emma and Jake taking the plunge, you would be next."

He doesn't take his eyes off the road when he replies, "I think she wants to. Hell, I think even I want to, but she's only halfway through her degree; I want to give her the chance to explore all her options before we go that far. I mean, I'm so much older than her, she's not had a chance to live yet and I wouldn't want her to regret settling down with me too soon. I've lived my wild life, sown my oats so to speak, so I think I know that I'm ready. I'm just giving her the chance to decide if she is."

"Sounds wise, but bro, I have to tell you…she's ready. You're blind if you can't see the hints she's been giving you."

He quickly turns to look at me, probably to see if I'm pulling his leg and when he can tell I'm serious, he returns his gaze to the road.

"You're right, I know, but Liv is impulsive at the best of times. I just want her to finish Uni, get herself the job of her dreams and then think about taking things to the next level between us. It's just a few years, I'm not saying never."

"Just don't go letting what you have slip through your fingers because you end up waiting too long. If it's right, it's right. Time is not going to change that."

He laughs, almost humourlessly, "When did you become the expert on all things relationship-related? I'm pretty sure you're still a virgin."

At his close to the mark comment, I burst into laughter, 'Yeah, with you, Jake, and even Isaac to some degree, being such whores, it's not surprising that you'd think me a virgin. Compared to you lot, I'm as pure as the driven snow."

A four-hour flight later, I touch down in the U.K. and a sense of rightness floods my veins.

This time, landing here, back in this country, feels like coming home and I can't wait to go and visit the two special girls who are responsible for that feeling.

If someone had told me that I, Liam Fox-Williams, would fall for not one sister but two and at the same time, I would have called them a fool.

But I have.

Each one has stolen a piece of me and claimed it for themselves and I cannot imagine not having them in my life.

I love them, it's simple.

I've confessed my love to Cari and she's said it back, but next time I need the words to come from her, no prompts and no more declarations from me. I need to know it comes from deep inside her and is not just a response she feels she has to give me.

three

I know she loved me then and I know she loves me now, but I still need to hear it from her; I need her to say the words before I do, even though I can feel them on the tip of my tongue every single time we speak. It's starting to hurt just trying to keep them from slipping out.

Less than two hours later, I'm back at my parents, where I don't bother to unpack, instead I rifle through my luggage and grab the gifts I bought for Cari and Seren.

I'm grateful no one is home. I love my Mum, I really do, but I don't have time for her to fuss over me right now. I have to go and see my girls.

It's teatime, so I know it should be safe to ring the doorbell without upsetting or waking Seren.

I probably should have called instead of just turning up here, but I want it to be a surprise.

I stand, in much the same position as I did that first time I knocked on this door and just like before, I spot Cari looking out of the side window in my peripheral vision.

The front door swings open and a split second later my small, fiery angel launches herself into my arms, almost making me drop the gifts in my hand.

I laugh into her hair, taking in her scent, "I guess this means you really missed me then?"

She pulls back to look at me then peppers my

face in small kisses, not missing an inch of skin.

"Just be quiet and let me kiss you."

Then she takes my mouth in a scorching hot kiss, the opposite of the feather light kisses she just placed all over my face. This kiss is fierce and immediately registers in my Foxson; yes, I did just adopt the same principle for naming my cock as H. I think it works well and can't wait to share his new name with Cari later. Her deep, throaty laugh, always makes him even harder and I know I'll hear it when I tell her the story behind the name.

A noise from the living room interrupts our doorstep make-out session and Seren comes barreling down the corridor with one of her PECs symbols in her hand.

I bend down to take it, "Hello, Seren," I quickly glance at the picture and word on the little card, "Do you want a biscuit?"

She replies by taking my hand and dragging me towards the kitchen where she thrusts me in front of the cupboard that houses her favourite treats.

I take one from the packet and turn to face her, bending down to her level once more. Having seen a little boy, very similar to Seren, on the beach with his parents in Ibiza, I use the technique I observed his mother doing with him. I bring the biscuit up to the side of my mouth and slowly and concisely say the word, "Biscuit," then hand it over to Seren who skips back into the living room clutching her treat in her hand.

three

Cari watches the whole scene from the doorway, a beautiful smile on her face. She strides towards me slowly, "Was that more 'Seren Wrangling' magic I just witnessed? Where did you see that before?"

I tell her all about the little boy and how I watched his parents do the same with any object he took an interest in and then I explain that on occasion I would hear him say the initial sound of the word, like "Shhh" for shell.

"I know it might not work for Seren, but figured it's easy enough to do and what with her saying 'soooos' more often, I figured she might be on the cusp of making more sounds."

Her hands wrap around my waist and she uses her small but somewhat mighty strength to pull me towards her, "Why don't you come here and give me a sws? I've missed those lips on mine."

I step towards her small frame and bend towards her mouth until her lips barely touch mine, "Why does that word sound so sexy coming from your mouth but not mine?"

She pulls back a little, seemingly perplexed by my question, "What word? Sws?"

I nod and she laughs, "It's because I'm Welsh and we're good with tongue-twisters while you English folk make them all sound like you're saying something rude."

I grin and then attempt to say something I heard once on TV, I think it's the longest place name ever or something, "Llanfairpwll…"

And there is that throaty laugh of hers that both me and my Foxson love so much, "What? Why are you laughing at me?" I ask with a straight face.

"Please, *please* do not attempt that word again. I was afraid you were going to hack some spit at me."

I try to look insulted but fail because I can't hold in my smile, "Don't take the piss out of my linguistic ability. You might upset my feelings."

"Oh, hush. You know damn well you just sounded like you were choking on your own tongue. Leave the Welsh to me, your job is to whisper sweet nothings in my ear not make me want to perform the Heimlich maneuver on you."

I purposely lower my voice aiming for seductive but probably failing, "Sweet nothings hey, why not come a little closer and give your man a 'soooos'. Or better yet, a full blown snog because one kiss isn't going to cut it."

"You say the sexiest things." There's humour in her voice, but I can also see her desire.

"God, I can't wait for bedtime…I mean that's if I'm invited for a sleepover tonight?"

She leans up on her tiptoes and places a gentle kiss on my mouth then speaks softly against my lips, "Did you really think I was going to let you leave tonight? I have plans for you that do not include learning any more Welsh words."

"Tell me more of these plans, I think I need to know what I'm getting into."

She smiles seductively, her tongue tracing my

three

bottom lip before she pulls away and looks me directly in the eyes, "Me. You're getting into me."

Fuck. I think my Foxson just exploded.

"Can you order enough for Laura-Nel too?"

I spin around to face Cari, my finger hovering over the dial button and my face obviously displaying my immediate surprise.

"What? You look like I've just told you the world is about to end. Don't panic, she's not coming over, she just loves eating day old Chinese food so I always order extra for her to have the next day."

Relief floods through me. The vision of spending my first night back with Cari, trying to charm her best friend into liking me, evaporates with her words and I let out a heavy breath.

"Panicked there for a moment, didn't you?"

She knows damn well I did, her eyes brightening with wickedness.

I hit dial on the phone and wait for it to connect, "You're going to pay for that Pritchard, I'm going to spank your pretty, little arse until…Oh, Hi…could I get the set meal for three please with an extra portion of chicken balls and some prawn crackers."

Cari cracks up with laughter and I give her the stink eye while telling the takeaway guy the address for delivery.

I hang up the phone and raise my eyebrows in challenge, "I think that spanking is coming your way sooner rather than later…" I look over at Seren who is happily playing with the new spinning, music box I bought for her from Ibiza, "Avert your eyes Seren, I'm about to teach your big sister a lesson."

I stalk towards Cari, who can see my intent and quickly darts behind the back of the sofa, trying to evade me. She feints left, but I read her move before she's even executed it and in less than three seconds, I've pinned her flat on the sofa underneath me, where I begin to tickle her relentlessly.

Between hiccups and strangled breaths, she forces out, "Liam…please…stop. I'm going to…pee myself."

It's not her words that make me stop, it's Seren, who wonders what the heck is going on and wants in on the action, diving on top of both me and Cari and using my back like her own personal trampoline.

This only makes Cari laugh louder.

"You think…oooof…that this is…humph… funny do you?"

Seren eventually slides off after her fun and games and skips back over to her music box. My back only just survives the attack and I roll off Cari and land with a thud on the floor between the sofa and the coffee table.

Cari leans over the edge of the sofa and peeks down at me, "That'll teach you for messing with a Pritchard girl, take on one of us and face the wrath of both."

I groan as I pull myself up, "I think I just figured that out and for a little slip of a girl, she sure attacks like she's twice her size. Well, my back feels like a

three

person twice her size has bounced all over it, put it that way." I wince and stand, stretching out my poor muscles which have taken a battering from Seren's knees and elbows.

"I need some TLC," I look down at a giggling Cari, "If you loved me you would be over here tending to my wounds, not giggling like a school girl."

Her giggles stop abruptly and I'm at a loss as to why.

She pushes herself up onto her elbows, her eyes locked on mine, "I do, you know."

I rub my lower back where Seren caught me with a particularly deathly blow, "Do what? Teach your sister violent ninja moves?"

Her eyes are no longer laughing, she looks nervous and yet determined, "Love you. You said if I loved you I would tend to you...and I need you to know that I do love you. So much."

She said it, she finally said it, albeit I let slip the word in an offhanded manner first.

We stare at each other for a long moment, my stunned reaction obviously putting her on edge as she begins to fiddle with her hair.

I shake away the shock and elation of finally hearing her say the words again and I'm about to bend and scoop her into my arms when the doorbell rings.

She jumps up from the sofa a little flustered, "The...ummm...that must be the takeaway."

She turns to walk towards the front door, but I know I can't let her walk away before addressing her confession. I catch up to her in just two strides, grab her just above the elbow and spin her around into my arms. She lets out a small gasp and then begins to protest, looking over her shoulder towards the door, "Liam, let me get the door…"

I cut off her words with my mouth, laying a fast but passionate kiss on her lips, "Fuck the door, you've just told me you love me, the delivery guy can wait." Then my mouth is back on hers, ravaging, taking and trying to swallow down the love she has just professed so that I can keep it deep inside me and it can never be taken away.

An insistent knock on the door followed by the doorbell ringing again breaks us apart.

"I love you too, more than I have the vocabulary to express."

She swallows at my words, her eyes becoming glassy with restrained tears. A third ring of the doorbell causes Seren to protest noisily and I know I have to let Cari go.

"I'll get the door, you set the table." I brush my thumb over her jaw and reluctantly let her go with one more soft kiss to her lips.

Just before I answer she calls to get my attention, "I should have said it sooner, I should have said it before. I was scared Liam, scared of losing you. I thought that if I didn't admit I loved you, then it would hurt less when I finally let you go."

three

She doesn't wait for my reply, she ducks quickly into the kitchen and I head straight to the door, hoping the delivery guy hasn't already left.

When I open it nobody is there, I glance up the street and I see him just about to get back into his car, our bag full of takeaway in his hand.

"Hey! Wait up!"

I apologise for not hearing him knock and give the bloke a healthy tip.

With the bag full of food in my hand, I jog back to the house, straight into the kitchen where Cari is busying herself with plates and cutlery.

Depositing the bag of food on the table, I waste no time in taking the silverware out of her hand and dumping it in a pile on the nearest surface.

I pull her into my arms, sweep back the hair she's allowed to fall into her face in an attempt to hide from me and lift her chin gently to force her to look into my eyes.

"When I told you I loved you a few years ago, I was just a teenage boy about to get his heart broken. I loved you with every part of my juvenile heart and even then I knew you loved me back. Now I stand before you, not as that young boy, but as a man; a man who still loves you with all his heart, but that love has evolved into so much more. What we have now is not a forbidden love, one conducted away from prying eyes. It's an open, honest love, one I am willing to tell the whole world about."

I cup her face gently and move my head closer to

hers, her emerald eyes bewitching me, telling me to come closer still.

"I've waited so long for you to open yourself up to me, for you to tell me what's in your heart. It didn't matter that I already knew, hearing you finally give me the last piece of your heart, has completely healed mine. I know you've lost so many people you've loved, but I promise…" I place a soft kiss on her lips, "…I promise you that you will never lose me. My fully healed heart and I agree, that you're it for us Cari. *You are my Cariad, my love.*"

The takeaway is long forgotten.

We stand locked in our embrace our bodies swaying slightly, seemingly moving to the synchronized beating of our hearts. A beat only our souls can hear in a dance that is only for us.

chapter 25

Cari

"We need to talk about your family." I break the comfortable silence we share at the table, in order to address something that is slowly churning around in my gut.

"When I bumped into your mother last week, I swear she could see my guilt, especially when my eyes bugged out of my head when she suggested telling you to get in touch with me."

I push my half-eaten Chinese food around my plate, thoughts of coming out to his parents as a couple, suddenly making me nauseous.

Seren's happy noises coming over the intercom from her bedroom are the only thing breaking the silence.

Liam leans over and takes away the fork that I've been using to make patterns in my food, placing it down on my plate and then grasping my now empty hand.

"Look at me."

His gentle command is impossible to ignore and when I lift my eyes to his, he begins to speak again, "There is no guilt, Cari. I was eighteen and old enough to make my own decisions. You did not take advantage of me, you were not preying on my naivety and youth. I mean, you're only a few years older than me anyway."

His thumb traces my knuckles and soothes away some of my worries, "But they won't see it that way if we tell them the whole truth. Hell, if I was your mother I think I'd want to throttle me."

He laughs, "You've not yet met my mother properly, trust me, when she sees how happy we are together, any thoughts of committing bodily harm will be long forgotten."

I huff, "Yeah, I'm not exactly convinced of my safety at this point. Plus, what if they hate me?"

He smiles and shakes his head, 'How could anyone hate you?"

"I corrupted you, Liam. I seduced their son when I was his teacher; I was the person paid to guide you and support you, instead I abused my position and had an affair with you. An affair that we both hid."

Steel fills his tone when he fires back, "You did not seduce me, I pursued you! Quite relentlessly if I remember rightly. I was young, but I wasn't a child, Cari. You have to remember that."

He softens his voice and continues, "If you want

three

me to tell them we've only just started our relationship, I will, but I'm not ashamed of our history and I'm not comfortable lying about it. We have nothing to hide, I wish you'd understand that."

I hesitate, still unsure if I can willingly let him introduce me as the teacher he previously had an affair with; one who, after meeting his parents that first night at the art show, then took him to a nearby hotel room and spent the night naked in his arms.

Then the following day, I tore out his heart by telling him it was over between us and that what we'd done was so very wrong.

I avert my eyes for a moment to gather my thoughts.

"What if we… maybe we could just, for now at least, say we've only just reconnected and if questions get asked about our history, we address them then?"

He sighs softly, "If that's what you want Cari, but I really want to take both you and Seren to meet my parents soon. My mother definitely knows I've come back to the U.K. for more than just the opportunity of a new job and the gallery space with Isaac. She knows I've met someone and she will keep pushing to find out who you are. Besides, I really want you to meet my family. They're a little crazy at times, well a lot actually, but I know they will be over the moon to finally meet the woman who has made me happier than they've seen me in such a long time. Plus, I'll give them the heads up about Seren, so they don't overwhelm her and I know they will fall in love with her too. I mean how can anyone not fall in love with her? She's beautiful, just like her big sister."

"Okay, take us to meet your family but let's just keep the past where it is for now. I'm nervous enough meeting them again as it is. The last time I was your teacher and this time I'll be your girlfriend."

He grins at me, my belly doing a flip at the happiness on his face, "My girlfriend... I *really* like it when you say that Cari. How long until Seren's bedtime because I really need to make love to my girlfriend right now and I don't think I can wait"

The wicked gleam in his eyes shows he's completely serious and I have to fight the urge to pounce on him and make him take me on the kitchen table.

I try and blow off how much his words have affected me with a shaky laugh, "It's only 5 o'clock, there are at least three hours until bedtime and she needs a bath and her supper."

He's up out of his chair and heading up the stairs before I can stop him, "Well, I'll start running the water, let's get operation 'Seren's bedtime' on the road."

"Hold up, eager beaver, she can't have a bath until she's had her physiotherapy. It's already on her schedule so she knows it's coming."

He pops his head around the bend in the stairs and looks back at me, "Well then, what are you waiting for? I'll run the bath a little hotter than usual, you go get bouncy on the gym ball with Seren and

three

then we'll be ready at the same time. Stop dilly-dallying; less chat, more teamwork."

I give him a little salute, "Yes, sir, on it, sir," and my flippant response makes him laugh.

"Oh baby, I love it when you call me Sir, maybe we can explore that a little later when Seren is finally in bed?" He winks and jogs back up the stairs.

A few moments later, I hear the water running and Liam singing something out of tune. It's a habit I've noticed he does when he's particularly happy and I find it endearing, even if his notes are flatter than a pancake.

I collect Seren's pink gym ball from the under-stairs cupboard and place it in the living room, moving the coffee table out of the way to create enough space.

When I get to her bedroom to collect her, I slowly open the door and find her lying next to the big bubble tube Liam bought and installed earlier today. A small square of sheer fabric from her sensory box is draped over her face and she's happily watching the bubbles while lying on her back with her feet in the air.

She doesn't even move when I enter the room, she is completely transfixed by her sensory heaven; the scrap of fabric over her eyes obviously adding another layer to her enjoyment of the bubbles and colours.

I walk over and lie down at her side, not touching but close enough that she's aware of my presence.

For a long moment, I drift away watching the soothing bubbles and think of the man who has given her this gift. A man who gives far more than he takes.

Seren turns her head to slowly look at me.

Eye contact from her is sporadic and often feels forced, the act of physically meeting someone's eyes appearing painful for her.

When her eyes meet mine it's almost an instinctual reaction to avert my gaze so she doesn't have to; so she can drink in my features without the stress of maintaining that contact she struggles with.

This time, I let her eyes linger on mine; emerald meets emerald and the effect it has on me is powerful.

She looks right at me, not at my hairline or the side of my nose; she looks deep into my eyes, hers softer and more open than I have ever seen them.

"Seren, sws?"

I'm greedy, I want more.

I want this connection, this rare tether that feels like delicate, gossamer spider's silk, to strengthen and grow.

She blinks but rolls to her side, her rosebud lips puckering to grant my request, her eyes still gently holding mine.

Her kiss is a gentle one, not typical of the full, wet smackers Seren normally gives and as soon as it's over she breaks our gaze and turns back towards the bubble tube.

three

This special moment gathers in my heart, spreads throughout my veins and pools in my eyes.

A minute later, I feel Liam lying down on the floor next to me. I turn my head to the side to see him watching Seren while his hand grips mine tightly.

I am no longer alone in life.

It is no longer just me and Seren.

We lie there, quietly watching the bubbles, three souls forever connected as one.

My past, my present and my future.

Liam, Cari and Seren.

Three.

chapter 26

Liam

When are u & J back home?

I stayed at my parents last night as it was one of Cari's evening classes and I know she likes to catch up with Laura-Nel afterwards.

I used the opportunity of having both my parents together, to tell them all about my budding relationship with Cari, how much I wanted to properly introduce her to them, her situation with Seren and how she is her sole custodian.

The story made my mother cry, although she did try to hide her tears.

She immediately wanted to know as much as possible about both Cari and Seren and eagerly wanted me to set a date for everyone to meet.

I hold her off by saying it's not as simple as just inviting them over, that things have to be put in place for Seren to cope and that's the reason I've just contacted Emma.

Their house is huge, has massive grounds with loads of trees and flowers and even has a pool which is securely hidden behind a large gated fence so Seren can only go in if accompanied by someone and wouldn't be able to gain entry on her own.

At least if I introduce everyone at once, in a place with plenty of space, Seren can hopefully feel a little less overwhelmed and I don't have to put them both through multiple visits in the future.

Cari and Seren's wellbeing is far more important to me than anything else.

Back in 2 days. Can't wait 2 catch up!

That means they will be home by Wednesday, so I'm sure she won't mind me asking her for a favour for the following weekend.

Want 2 introduce Cari & Seren 2 the fam. Figured your place would make the perfect venue. Fancy helping your new bro out?

Yes, it's a little cheeky, but my Jules has always had difficulty telling me no.

Sure! I'll call when we get back 4 more details & find out what things I can get 2 make the visit less stressful for Seren. So happy you've worked things out and are

ready 2 come out of the shadows together. Can't wait 2 meet them both!

God, I love this girl.

My brother is one lucky bastard to have married her.

Thanks, Jules. Ur a star! I owe u big time!

Don't worry Li, I plan on collecting ;)

I briefly wonder if I should check with Cari before making plans, but figure I'll discuss it with her later. If the coming weekend doesn't work, I know Emma will be fine with rearranging.

I quickly call Isaac to see if he can make it and also send a text to Josh and Nate. I consider inviting H, but his larger than life personality might be too much for this visit, so I shelve that idea and head downstairs to let my mother know the plans.

I find her in the kitchen, ingredients strewn everywhere, notebooks littering the counter and an old Polaroid camera hanging from her neck.

"Do you think you could make any more mess?"

Her head pops up and I see smears of flour and other foodstuffs across her face. I've never seen my mother so bedraggled.

"It's the bloody WI cookbook I've signed up to take part in. None of these recipes are mine, but I have to make them so Isaac can photograph them.

three

Trouble is, half of these instructions are illegible; the other half describe concoctions that will end up truly inedible."

Seeing her so flustered when she's always so composed, especially in her main domain of the kitchen, forces me to offer to help, even though I am useless in the kitchen and would probably burn water.

"Need some help? How about if I tidy up a little, then make you a cuppa and you can tackle the recipes with renewed vigor."

She huffs some stray hairs out of her face, unhooks the camera from around her neck and sits herself down on a stool, "If you did that for me I will declare you my favourite son. Just don't tell your brothers."

I can't help but chuckle and I move over to the sink to fill up the kettle before making a start on the mess that covers almost every flat surface.

"So... How would you feel about meeting Cari and Seren this weekend at Jake and Emma's?"

My back is towards her, but I know I have her full attention.

"I would tell you, as my now favourite son, that I can't wait to meet them. Then I would ask how I could make the situation easier for them both, particularly Seren."

I turn my head to look over my shoulder and find her staring at me with a wide smile on her face.

"Thanks, Mum. What would make it easier is if you let everyone know to keep things pretty subdued and not to crowd them both. I'll make sure there are things in place that Seren will enjoy and Jules has promised help with, but unlike other children who you naturally want to fuss over, you can't do that with Seren. So just a quick hello will be more than enough. I'm sure once you've spent some time with her, you'll soon see how to adapt and make things less stressful for her."

"So…less is more."

"Yes, when it comes to how the Fox-Williams' normally are, in this case, less is most definitely more."

"Leave it with me, I'll make sure everyone understands. I think we are so eager to meet them both that we'd likely scare off even the most tolerant of people, it won't hurt for us to turn the volume down on our excitement."

The kettle boils and I quickly make her tea, placing the hot mug in front of her a few moments later.

"I'm happy to have you home, but I'm even happier to see you in love. She must be very special to have stolen my baby boy's heart."

I stop wiping up the spilt flour and lean on the counter to look at her, "She is special. So special, she doesn't even realise it."

My mother gives me a knowing look and replies, "The best people never do."

three

It takes well over an hour to clean up the kitchen and by the time we've finished, she no longer feels like trying again.

"Stuff this, I'm going to go and have a long, hot soak in the bath and then inform your father that he can take me out for dinner tonight. Would you like to join us?"

"No thanks, I'm just going to grab a quick shower and then spend the night over at Cari's. In fact..." I glance up at the kitchen clock, "I promised I'd be there around now, so I'd better get a move on."

She walks towards me and wraps up my big body in one of her squeezy hugs, "Thanks for saving me today. If you hadn't, I dread to think what state I would have continued to get myself in. I think it's time to pack up this cookbook malarkey and go back to cooking for fun."

"If you're not enjoying it anymore, I agree, don't do it. You've already proved yourself in your field. Start enjoying an early retirement, make Dad take you on that around-the-world trip. You don't have to be here for us anymore, it's time to live life for you again and not for us."

She loosens her arms around me and looks up at my face, "When did my baby boy get so wise?"

I grin down at her, "When I started listening to the wisest woman I know."

Less than an hour later, I text Cari to let her

know I'm outside.

I'm here & I've got chocolate cake

The cake is my mother's doing. She practically forced the freshly cooked creation on me, saying it was the only thing worth salvaging from her disastrous afternoon in the kitchen and seeing as she was going out, someone needed to enjoy the fruits of her labour.

Mere moments after hitting send, the front door swings open and a tall, willowy blonde, with ice blue eyes, opens the door with a scowl on her face.

She looks me up and down before her eyes settle on the covered cake stand in my hands.

"Well, seeing as you brought cake, I think I'll let you in."

"Laura-Nel...stop winding him up and let him in." Cari's voice calls out from inside the house, her head appearing over Laura-Nel's shoulder a few moments later, "Oh yummy, you brought cake."

She sidesteps around her friend and stretches onto her tiptoes to kiss me on the cheek. I've yet to say a word because Laura-Nel is still giving me the stink eye and blocking my entry.

Cari turns and follows my gaze, "Laura-Nel, pack in it. Stop trying to intimidate him."

Her friend's icy gaze sparkles with mirth and she bends over in a full belly laugh, "You should have seen his face, it was bloody priceless."

three

Cari slaps her friend across the shoulder and taking my hand, pulls me through the door behind her. I'm not sure what the joke is or maybe her friend is a few sandwiches short of a picnic, whatever is going on, I haven't got the foggiest.

Cari carefully takes the cake from me and sets it on the table, lifting off the cover to reveal the chocolate creation beneath.

"My mother baked it and wanted me to bring it over for you."

I'm suddenly feeling really shy and a little awkward. Cari gives me a grateful smile and is about to speak when Laura-Nel slides her hand under the open cover and swipes her finger through the chocolate frosting.

She brings it to her mouth and overdramatically moans around the digit that she's currently sucking and licking with gusto.

"Enough with the porn star groans; I know you're trying to embarrass Liam. Behave, you've had your fun. It's time to play nice." Cari chastises her, but all Laura-Nel does in reply is lean towards the cake for a second helping.

The resounding slap Cari gives her hand is enough to make me startle and Laura-Nel holds the now stinging appendage against her chest as if to protect it from further attack.

'Hey, that wasn't nice. He's a big boy now, he can take a little teasing."

"I've told you to stop referring to him as a boy

and I don't mind a little teasing but look at him," she motions her hand in my direction, "he's beetroot red and doesn't know where to look."

I clear my throat, "I'm right here you know."

Two sets of eyes turn my way, "It's umm…nice to meet you, Laura-Nel. Cari's told me so much about you, but she neglected to tell me that you do voiceovers for the premium rate sex lines."

Oh shit.

I've just insulted her best friend and the person that's been trying to yank my chain since I turned up.

I glance from one to the other, Laura-Nel's mouth is gaping wide open while Cari grins mischievously.

I fluster a little trying to backtrack, "I…what I mean is…"

Loud laughter erupts from both women simultaneously and they both point in my direction while trying to catch their breath through their giggles.

"Oh, you're just adorable and you can give as good as you get. You'll suit my girl perfectly."

Laura-Nel strides across the room and wraps me in a tight bear hug.

I stand rigidly, not knowing if I should return her hug, or if laying my hands on her might get me a slap because this is another one of her weird tests. I look over her shoulder at a still hysterical Cari and plead with my eyes for her to help me.

"I'm so sorry for not warning you…Laura-Nel

likes to…test people before she can make friends with them. Seems like you've just passed."

She eventually releases me and pats me across the cheek like a grandmother would a small child, "Nice to finally meet you, Liam. I'm sorry for the chocolate-gasm, but it was necessary to test your mettle. My girl is feisty and I had to make sure you could keep up."

Then, she strolls out of the kitchen towards the living room, calling over her shoulder, "Put the kettle on big boy and bring me in a slice of cake while I go and check on Serendipity."

Cari is still laughing, but trying to control it better and she shakes her head at the retreating form of her friend.

"Come give me a sws, big boy. You deserve it after that welcome."

She bats her eyelashes at me in mock innocence.

"Uh-uh, I'm not touching you with that crazy bird around. You could have warned me I was walking into a trap. I didn't even know I was meeting her today."

"Where would the fun be in that," she walks towards me, no hint of remorse given, "besides, I'm meeting your parents soon. I'm sure that's going to be far worse than what you've just endured."

I wince, deciding there's no time like the present, "Actually… you'll be meeting everyone, including my brothers and their significant others, this weekend at Jake's house."

This news stops her in her tracks, "You...what?"

"Emma and Jake have invited us to their place this weekend, along with the rest of my family. They can't wait to meet you both."

Her face pales, "You want me...and Seren, who by the way doesn't do well in new environments, to not only meet your parents this weekend but also your brothers? The house in which all this will take place is Jake's? Who also happens to be a huge star, does that about sum it all up?"

I hold out both hands in a placating gesture and slowly walk towards her, "It's not as bad as it sounds, trust me they will love you both and Jake's not a star to us, he's just Jake. Plus, Seren will love their place, they have a huge garden spanning their property that is filled with trees and flowers, she'll be in her element. That's why I thought it would be a better idea than going to my parents' place."

She looks down at the floor, all trace of her previous humour gone, "I...I don't know. I'm not sure Seren will cope."

I take another step forward and hold both her fidgeting hands in mine.

"Stop. Please don't use Seren as an excuse."

"I...I wasn't!" Her voice gains strength with her adamant denial.

I step even closer until our bodies are flush and her hands rest against my chest, "Do you trust me?" She nods. "Then trust me enough not to put Seren, or you, in a situation that will cause either of you distress. I promise I've got this covered."

"Oh, for heaven's sake! Either snog his face off or put the boy down and make me a cup of tea. I'm parched in here."

We both turn to the doorway to see Laura-Nel staring at us with her hands on her hips, "Oh, and even I can see he would never lead you or Seren into a minefield, so stop making excuses and go and meet his rels." She turns and then changes her mind mid-step, turning to look directly back at me, "Oh, and big boy, how about you get me your hot as sin brother's autograph on a nude piccie if possible. I'm sure his new wife won't mind; she seems lovely when she's interviewed on TV."

I choke on a laugh and shoot back quickly, "I'll get you a signed picture if you stop calling me big boy."

She eyes me skeptically, "Nude?"

I laugh around my words, "Give me a break, he's my brother for Christ's sake. I can promise a selection of signed photos in various forms of dress, perhaps with a bit of bared chest. Do we have a deal?"

I hold out my hand for her to shake and she looks down at it thoughtfully before meeting my eyes and spitting on her open palm, "Deal."

I stare in disgust at the proffered hand and she begins to laugh at me again, "Don't worry, big boy, I didn't actually spit on it so shake my hand and if you hold up your end of the deal, I promise to never to call you big boy again."

I look into her face to test her honesty and reluctantly reach out for her hand, thankfully it's dry. While shaking it quite vigorously, she adds, "I'll call you little man instead."

Then she turns and leaves us once more.

I stare at the empty doorway for a second, wondering if I'll ever get used to how kooky she is and then thinking of the car crash that would happen if she were ever to meet H.

"She's right you know."

Cari's soft rasp brings my attention back to her, "I'm being stupid. I know you'd never do anything to upset me or Seren. I'm just nervous, I guess and was hoping to put it off for a little while longer."

I turn and pull her back into my arms, kissing her forehead, followed by her closed lids, then her lips, "I can't wait for them to meet you. Thank you for saying yes."

"She opens her eyes and looks up at me, "With you, I don't think I'm capable of saying no."

"Can I have a blowjob?" she smacks me hard across the stomach, "I'm kidding, I'm kidding. After the experience you just put me through with your crazy friend, I had to get my own back somehow."

I know I'm forgiven when she looks up at me, tracing the dimple in my cheek that pops out when I grin, "I love you, Liam."

I close my eyes on a sigh, "I'll never get tired of hearing you say that." Then I snog her face off as I was recently directed to by her batty best friend.

chapter 27

Cari

It's Saturday.

The day we will meet the entire Fox-William clan.

I feel sick.

So sick, I wonder if I can call up Liam and beg off today.

"I can see exactly what you're thinking and *no* I am not letting you pike out of going today."

Seren is in her bedroom because it has quickly become her favourite place to be since Liam bought her a bubble tube of her own and Laura-Nel and I are in my bedroom, tearing apart my limited wardrobe, trying to find something suitable for me to wear.

I've already showered and pinned back my hair, I've even applied mascara and a little loose powder.

I hope Liam appreciates my efforts.

"I wasn't going to say that… I was going to say…" She turns to face me, a pair of torn jeans in one hand and a *Kasabian* t-shirt in the other.

"I can read you like an open book, don't lie to me Cari Pritchard," she looks at the garments in her hands and scrunches up her face in disgust, "Are the only things you own jeans and band tees?"

I nod up at her from my fetal position on the bed.

"Do you not own a dress or even a pretty top that doesn't look washed out or contain a logo?" she bends and scoops up two different coloured Converse. "And don't get me started on your shoes. You only own trainers!"

"I'm too short for dresses, most drown me and make me look like a little girl who's raided her mother's wardrobe."

She rolls her eyes and continues to dig through what's left of my clothes, "That's what petite departments are for. They cater for little people like you; you know, the vertically challenged."

"Ha bloody Ha, I've got nothing to wear so why don't you just let me phone Liam and tell him I have the lurgy."

"No. Suck it up buttercup. We've got over an hour before he comes to get you. That's more than enough time for me to run down to the high street, hit *Topshop* and get back here to help you dress."

I flop back down on the bed in defeat.

"Great. You're such a good friend."

She leans over my sulking form, places a wet kiss on my cheek and then pats over the top, "I know I

three

am. You'd be lost without me. Now get up before you make a mess of your hair."

"Yes, boss."

Less than forty minutes later she's back with a choice of three outfits and I have to admit, they are all pretty cute.

One is a vintage looking tea dress with a cute lace trim, but what makes it a little quirkier is hidden amongst the abundance of flowers are small silver skulls that you have to be really up close to notice.

The second outfit comprises of an ankle length, pale pink, paisley skirt, with a plain white, ribbed vest and attached to the vest is a stunning jade necklace detail.

The final outfit is skinny jeans and a floral blazer.

I quickly try on each outfit and surprisingly love them all.

"You can shop for me all the time. Your skills are wasted working on reception at the dentist."

"I know, I know, it's a travesty dahhhlingg…" she replies like one of the fashion elite, "Now I think you should wear the skirt and vest, that way you can throw on your denim jacket, the pink Converse and you've not compromised your personal style. I don't want you to feel even more uncomfortable and unsure of yourself than you already do."

I quickly redress in the second outfit, adding my pink Converse and shrugging my denim jacket over the top.

"And take the pins out your hair, that look needs

your wild locks free."

I hesitate, staring at myself in the mirror and actually liking what I see, "Are you sure?"

"Yes. I'm sure. Now get a jig on, I'll go and make sure Seren has everything in her bag and then head home so you can prepare her for today's adventure."

Before she walks through the door, I run over and wrap her in a hug.

"You're right, as always. I'd be lost without you."

"I know."

I laugh into her hair, "Is there anything that you don't know?"

"Nope."

"Well, in that case, I'm also grateful for your unequalled intellect and knowledge, but most of all I'm grateful that you're my best friend."

"Stop, before you make me cry. It's my time of the month and my eyes tend to leak more for some reason. Hormones I guess."

I hug her a little tighter before letting her go.

"Hormones hey? Nothing to do with the fact that you're a big softy?"

"Nope," she sniffles and then heads out of the door, stopping on the threshold to remind me, "Don't forget, big boy promised me signed piccies. You make sure he delivers."

"How could I possibly forget? You've already reminded me a dozen times since you arrived this morning."

three

"Well, now I'm reminding you again. I want chest, abs and hopefully a money shot, at the least I expect a happy trail."

"You're incorrigible, now get going before you make me late."

I hear Laura-Nel leave at the same time Liam arrives. I can hear her remind him about his promise before she shouts out, "Toodle Pip, bitches." And then flounces out the house.

I hear Liam's laughter as he climbs the stairs, muttering to himself "she is one crazy bird."

I hear him opening Seren's door quietly and peeking in, then he closes it and his footsteps head in my direction.

Butterflies take flight in my stomach; the closer his footfalls come, the more their tiny wings flutter in nervous excitement.

Moments later, he's in my doorway; his eyes running from the top of my head to the tips of my shoes.

"Wow. You look incredible."

He stalks towards me with heat in his eyes.

"Not that I don't love your band t-shirts and jeans but I've never seen you in a skirt and I have to admit I'm liking the thought of the easy access it provides."

He reaches out and places his hands on my

shoulders, then skims them down over my arms before he finds my fingers and links his with mine.

"Are you ready for today?"

"As I'll ever be."

His hands squeeze mine, "They are all going to fall in love with you, just like I already have. Jules is so excited to meet you that I've had to reign in her enthusiasm a little. She's even hired a travel sensory room that's housed in a mini-bus so Seren has somewhere to escape if it all gets a bit too much for her."

My eyes widen at the generosity of a woman who has yet to meet me or my sister, "Wow. That's so thoughtful of her…I…umm wish she hadn't gone to so much trouble, though. Seren would be just as happy in the garden I'm sure."

"Jules never does things by halves. Did you remember to put both your swimsuits in Seren's bag just in case she wants to go in the pool?"

"Yes, I've put them in, along with her iPad and some of her puzzles just in case. Can I ask why you call her Jules if her name is Emma?"

He smiles and quickly tells me the story of how they met and the reason for her nickname.

"She sounds amazing, no wonder you guys hit it off so well."

I try to keep any hint of jealousy out of my words, but he obviously picks up on it when he reassures me, "She's my best friend and like a sister to me. Well, technically she is my sister now. There was never anything between us. I was and always will be, hooked on you."

'I wasn't…I didn't mean…"

"I'm just setting things straight in case you ever wonder. We have a close relationship, Jules and I; my brother, who is the most possessive person I've ever come across, especially in regards to Jules, knows we've never shared anything more than friendship, I just need you to know that too."

"I love you."

Everything he does is with me in mind.

What did I do right to deserve a second chance with this amazing and completely selfless man?

"I love you too, now let's go and do some 'Seren wrangling' so we're not late. My mother is a stickler for punctuality."

My eyes widen and I glance at the clock, he catches my worry and laughs, "She couldn't care less if we're late as long as we turn up. I'm sorry for teasing you. I promise I won't tease you again until I get you alone tonight."

His words are laced with a sensual promise and I can feel my cheeks heat, "That's not helping to calm my nerves you know."

He stops to feather his fingers over the redness on my cheeks, "I've got you. You don't ever need to feel nervous because I've *always* got you."

chapter 28

Liam

Seren is in a very compliant mood today and happily gets into the car for the thirty-minute journey to Jake and Emma's place.

I hold Cari's hand the entire way, only letting go to change gears.

I hope the simple touch will help calm her nerves, but the closer we get to our destination, the more restless I feel her getting and a few minutes before we arrive, she drops my hand and starts fidgeting with the ends of her long hair.

I pull over in a side street, no more than a mile away from Jake's and turn to face her.

"Hey, look at me."

She ignores my request and keeps fiddling with her hair.

The fact the car has stopped confuses Seren, who loudly protests about our lack of movement.

"Cari, please, I don't want to hang around and

three

risk upsetting Seren, so please, look at me."

She turns her head my way but keeps her eyes downcast.

"Give me those emerald greens, I need to see what you're feeling and you have such expressive eyes that they always allow me a glimpse into your thoughts."

When her gaze connects with mine I see just how anxious she has become.

"Listen," I reach out and retake one of her hands, "If we get there and you hate it, if someone makes you uncomfortable or if Seren hates it and doesn't cope, then we just leave. No one will think badly of us, they know how hard this is for you both."

She startles and I rush to change my wording, "No, no. I don't mean they know about our past, well Jules does, but she won't say a word, I mean everyone knows it might be a short visit if Seren gets upset and they know how difficult it is for you to even attempt this today because of it."

She latches onto the one part of the sentence that I instantly regret saying, "Emma knows? About us? About our affair?"

I can feel her nerves escalate when her hands start to shake, I need to fix this and fast, "She does, but only because like I told you before, she's my best friend. I had to talk to someone about you and Jules is the least judgmental person you will ever meet. She's such a strong person and reminds me a lot of you in that way."

She opens her mouth and I realise I have possibly made another blunder, "I mean she reminds me of you because you've both waded through the pain life has thrown at you and come out the other side with scars that have only made you stronger, not weaker."

Her hands slowly still and Seren's noises from the back seat get a little louder, she even throws in a kick in for good measure.

"I think Miss Seren needs to go, are you good, *are we good?*"

She squeezes my hand before re-lacing our fingers, "We're more than good. I'm sorry for my freak out. I just want them to see me as Cari and not your old teacher."

"They will, I promise. Now let's get going before my brothers eat all the food. My mother always makes the best finger food."

I have to let her hand go to pull back onto the road, but as soon as I can, I reach over and clasp it in mine again.

"I've got you."

When I look over she smiles at me, her nerves all but gone, "And I've got you."

I've already briefed everyone not to make a huge fuss when we arrive, so when we pull up Jake's long driveway and park directly outside his house, there is no fanfare to greet us and for that I am truly grateful.

I turn to look at Seren, who is busy staring out

of her window at the large, weeping willow tree that sits in the centre of the turning space. Her hands flap excitedly as she watches the long, trailing branches, blow gently in the breeze.

When I look back at Cari she is already watching me, "You really do love her don't you?"

I maintain our connection so I can emphasise my words, "As if she were my own."

"Thank you." Her eyes are overflowing with sincerity.

"Don't thank me for something that comes as naturally to me as breathing."

"I can thank you for loving us and I will continue to thank you for the rest of my days."

I smile and bring her hand up to place a soft kiss on her palm, "I like that... *the rest of our days.*"

We gather up Seren's bag, which is extra full today as we wanted to be prepared for every eventuality and help a rather excited, little girl from the car.

She immediately shrugs her hand out of mine, side steps Cari with lightening fast moves that I've never seen before and skips over to the willow tree.

My heart beats frantically in my chest and I mentally berate myself for not having had a better hold of her. If we were on a main road, that could have ended in tragedy.

"Don't beat yourself up, she evaded me too. Why do you think we avoid busy roads and crowded areas? If Seren has her sights set on something, she is relentlessly sneaky."

Cari appears at my side and I lean in to wrap my arm over her shoulder.

"I need to find some kind of reins or safety straps for her to make sure she's safe when you're walking. I'll do some research later, I bet they have them on the internet somewhere."

She snuggles into my side as we watch the little girl who has stolen both our hearts and also makes them race with worry.

"I love you, Liam Fox-Williams."

"I love you, Cari Pritchard."

She grasps my hand and tugs me towards the little girl who is currently running her hands through the low hanging branches of the tree. "C'mon, let's get 'Seren Wrangling', it's time we went inside; I can feel at least three sets of eyes staring holes into my back."

I chuckle lightly and turn to see if she's correct. She tugs on my arm roughly, "No! Don't bloody look, just entice Seren away from that tree and let's get this over and done with before I do a runner."

I laugh under my breath, "I bet it's only my mother, Jules and Liv. I guarantee all the men are out the back sinking beers and playing pool."

She grits her teeth and smiles at me, "I don't care who it is, what I do care is the longer we stay out here, the more I'm going to want to get back in your car and drive far away."

"Okay, okay. Go and make sure you've got

three

everything out of the car and I'll give our girl her five-minute countdown."

I pull my phone out of my pocket and activate the visual timer we now use on a regular basis, especially when out and about.

It works a treat and Seren happily takes my hand when the five minutes are up and skips along with me to the side of the house.

"Shouldn't we knock?" Cari looks at me warily.

"Why would we knock when we know everyone will be around back? C'mon scaredy cat, even Miss Seren is excited to see what's going to happen next."

I reach my free hand out and offer it to her, she holds it instantly and I give hers a small squeeze. We round the corner and begin to hear the voices of my family chatting away. The sound makes Cari tense up a little so I catch her eye and whisper, "I've got you."

The smile she gives me is small, but it's still a smile and I hope this day goes well so I can see that smile get bigger.

"Mr. and Mrs. Fox-Williams, it's really lovely to see you again."

Cari leans in to give them both a kiss on the cheek while I stand next to Seren who has taken great interest in one of the garden wind chimes.

"Please call me Honor and this is Max. Liam tells us that your first name means love, do you prefer

Cari or Cariad? I've never heard such a pretty name before."

"Everyone calls me Cari, my mother only ever called me Cariad if I was being naughty."

She smiles, begins to relax into the conversation and I feel my shoulders drop with relief.

Jules appears at my side with a bottle of beer and nods towards Seren who is happily running her fingers through the wind chime, "She looks happy," she hands over the cold Peroni and continues, "why don't I keep Seren company and you can go check on your girl."

I look around to see Cari chatting away to my mother, she seems relaxed, but I'm sure she'd much rather I was at her side.

"Thanks, Jules, if you need me just give me a shout. If she gets bored of this, you can always take her over to the trees. This huge garden of yours is like paradise for our little outdoors girl."

"We'll be fine, now go and keep Cari company, I can see Isaac heading her way and you know he'll tell her all sorts of stories about you if you're not there to defend yourself."

I lean in and place a kiss on her cheek, "You're going to make a great mother, Jules," I throw her a wink as I walk away, "so hurry up and make me an uncle."

She laughs out loud, "Oh, trust me, your brother is working on it."

"TMI, Jules. Too much bloody info."

three

"So, did Li-Li tell you about the time he got his winky stuck in the zip of his school trousers?" Isaac waits until he sees me approach before he loudly asks her this question. His devious grin telling me he was waiting for the right moment to spread this lie.

I wrap my arms around Cari from behind, linking them around her small waist and lean my head on her shoulder.

"He's an out and out liar, don't believe a word he says. I got my pants stuck in the zip of my school trousers, which stopped me from being able to undo them and caused me to pee myself. I was five at the time."

I feel her shoulders move with laughter, "Aww, poor little Li-Li."

She pats my hands, "Did little Li-Li finally get his zip fixed?"

Isaac grins at me, loving the fact she has joined in the teasing.

I whisper seductively in her ear, low enough only she can hear me, "Calling me Li-Li is worse than calling me, big boy. Unless you want that spanking I've promised you a few times, you'd better stop and behave yourself."

She swallows audibly and I know my words have affected her. Isaac, wondering what I've just said to provoke such a reaction, looks at me with what could only be described as awe, "Well, Li-Li, it seems you've developed moves I never even knew you were capable of."

I grin with pride, but Cari clears her voice and supplies, "Oh, you are *so* right. Li-Li has moves that would blow your mind."

Isaac laughs, takes a swig from his beer bottle and then tips it towards her, "Oh, you and me are going to get along just fine."

I playfully bite her shoulder and she gives out a small yelp, drawing the attention of everyone else around us and causing her face to burn with embarrassment.

Through gritted teeth that she tries to hide behind a smile, she turns towards me and threatens, "Your Foxson is going to be grounded for the foreseeable future if you continue."

I kiss her heated cheeks and reply, "Oh, my Foxson is a persuasive fellow, I'm sure he can worm his way into your knickers."

She smiles, evil delight in her eyes, "Are you sure you want to use the word worm in connection to your Foxson?"

I shrug, "Baby, you and I both know there is nothing worm-like about him."

"Are you gonna introduce me to your girl, or do I have to do so myself?"

Jake appears just behind Cari and I feel her startle a little when she recognises his voice.

three

I turn her in my arms but never let her go, "Cari, this is my whore-bag brother, Jake. J this is Cari."

Like the womanizer he is, or was prior to Jules, and probably to get a rise out of me, he takes her hand and leans down to kiss the back of it.

"Hell, if all my teachers looked like you when I was in school, I'd have popped my cherry a hell of a lot sooner."

Cari goes ridged in my arms, "Fuck off, bro. You screwed half the school, you didn't need to add the teachers to your list."

I hope my humour diverts him from making any more, hot teacher jokes. I can feel Cari wanting to make a run for it and he's not helping the situation.

"I guess you have a point," he winks at Cari and then continues, "So, you're the reason this little wanderer has returned? I know Emmy and Mum are ecstatic to have him around again."

Her voice is a little shaky when she responds, "I'm not sure I'm the only reason."

He smiles his trademark smile, "I'm guessing you're the most important reason."

Turning his attention to me, he adds, "So, you're setting up with Isaac? That's a good fit for you bro. I'd like to hire you for a project actually. Emmy loves your art, can I commission a wedding portrait from you? I've told Iz to let you have full access to all the wedding photos."

Warmth fills my chest at his request, "I'd be honoured. Let me get settled into my new place and

I'll start on it straight away."

He nods his thanks, "You found somewhere yet?"

I feel Cari turn to watch me and it makes me aware I've not yet discussed this with her, "Nah, bro. I've not had a chance to look yet, but I can't stay home with Mum and Dad forever, I like my own space too much."

"Amen to that. I love Mum but, fuck me, she drives me crazy sometimes."

"I hear you. She's been pretty good about me moving out, though. Maybe you, Nate and Josh have paved the way for us younger ones and she's able to come to terms with it quicker."

His eyes stray behind me and I can tell he's looking over at Seren and Jules who are now walking through the garden, inspecting every flower they come across.

Longing fills his eyes and Cari also turns to see what has caught his attention, "She's so good with her. I can tell she's going to be the most amazing mother. Are you thinking of starting a family?" She laughs and shakes her head, "I mean…not that it's any of my business. I forget you're famous and probably get asked questions like this all the time."

He smiles genuinely at her and then looks back to his wife, "Every time I look at her I start thinking about making babies, but seeing her, happily wandering around with that beautiful little girl of yours, I all but have to force myself not to go over

three

there, throw her over my shoulder and tell all of you lot to piss off home."

I shake my head, but Cari laughs loudly, her rasp almost coming back in full force, "Despite the delivery, I think that's one of the most romantic things I've ever heard."

Jake doesn't reply, his eyes are still tracking his wife and after downing the rest of his bottle, he makes his excuses and heads over to her.

I pull Cari to me and we watch Jake randomly picking flowers and offering them to Seren. Each one he picks, she then tries to eat and both myself and Cari chuckle at Jules trying her hardest to keep them from going into her mouth.

After a few hours of catching up with my family, Seren having fun in both the pool and the sensory-mobile that Jules hired for the afternoon, we say our goodbyes knowing that a tired little girl will be harder to get home than one that is still happy.

"Thanks for having us, Emma and Jake. I think Seren has had more fun today than I've ever seen her have before."

Cari and Jules had hit it off immediately and have spent the majority of the day together along with Liv, Laura, baby Ivy and my mother.

All the women easily forming bonds while all us men have spent hours just shooting the shit.

"Don't thank me, I think it's the most fun I've had in a long time too. We'd love you all to visit again soon, so don't be a stranger, okay? You've got my number so when you're free for a coffee just let me know."

Emma wraps Cari in a hug and then proceeds to pass her around all the other females to do the same.

When I get a chance, I lean in to give her a kiss on the cheek, "Thanks for today, Jules. I know Seren only coped and had such a good time because of you and everything you set up to make this day a special one for her. I owe you big time."

She bats me away with her hand and then steps back into Jake's embrace.

"I'm going back to Canada to begin filming season two tomorrow and Emmy is staying here for a few days before she joins me; take care of my woman while I'm gone. I know you both have the cheque presentation day for the school tomorrow and I'm counting on you to make sure the paparazzi don't hound my wife."

"You know I'll always look out for her. Good luck with the filming and don't let all the fame go to your head now."

He snorts and Isaac butts in, "It's already gone to his head, well the one in his pants at least."

Jules playfully smacks him across the back and Cari finally comes to stand at my side, "Behave yourself, Iz, you know he's a one-woman man now, he's got the ring to prove it."

three

"Too right," Jake all but growls, pulling Jules tightly back against his chest.

Cari motions to where Seren and my mother are playing with the wind chimes that first caught her attention early today, "I think we'd better get going, a tired Seren is no fun at all. Thanks again for today. I'll see most of you tomorrow. Have a safe flight, Jake."

We make our way towards my mum and Seren and thankfully our happy little girl is content to leave with very little persuasion.

The ride home is a happy but relatively silent one while we all reflect on how well today went.

When we arrive back, Cari turns to face me as I pull up to the curb outside their house.

"I'm sorry for stressing about today. Everyone was so welcoming and I think Seren had the best day of her life."

I turn off the engine and twist in my seat to face her, "I'm not going to say I told you so, but..."

"Don't even say it or else I might still refuse your Foxson any action."

"My lips are sealed." I zip my fingers across my mouth and motion throwing away the key.

She laughs, "C'mon, funny boy. Let's get this tired little girl settled and ready for bed. If you're really good, you might get a reward."

I turn to look at Seren, still sat quietly in her car

seat. She yawns and scrunches her eyes together as if to ward off the sleep that is threatening her.

"C'mon then, Miss Seren. How about a quick story before bedtime?"

I sit down next to her on the floor by her bubble tube and begin reading aloud from *Snow White*.

I picked the book up a few days ago because the image on the cover, reminded me so much of the little girl I was on my way to visit.

This is the first time I've tried to read it to her and I hope she'll let me while she watches her bubbles.

"Once upon a time in midwinter, when the snowflakes were falling like feathers from heaven…"

At first, she seems to pay me no attention but about a third of the way through the story she stops watching the bubbles and starts watching me.

By the time the story is over, she is sitting by my side, looking at all the pictures while I read the words.

I shut the book just in time to see Cari leaning up against the door watching us, "Seren," she waits for her to turn towards her voice, "Wash time now, then bed."

Seren gets up from the floor, using my shoulder to help her and dutifully walks towards Cari.

It's not often she complies immediately but when she does, you almost forget for a second that

three

this is not the norm.

Cari takes her hand and guides her towards the bathroom, looking over her shoulder as she walks away, "I've just taken a bottle of wine out of the fridge if you want to pour us some. I shouldn't be too long."

I stand and bow in her direction, causing a smile to break out on her face, "Your wish is my command, madam."

"You should read fairytales more often, I kinda like this Prince Charming routine you've got going on."

"Yes, M'lady." I bow once more and head down the stairs, eager to finally get some one on one time with my woman.

Around twenty minutes later, Cari tiptoes down the stairs and stands in the doorway of the living room, "Bring the bottle and both glasses with you and I'll meet you in the bedroom, I just want to have a quick shower."

I stand and go to bow again, she stops me with a quiet giggle, "Enough with the bowing, just get yourself, your Foxson and that wine in my bed right now."

"God, I love it when you're bossy."

I dart as if to chase her up the stairs, but stop when I realise there is no quiet way to pursue her.

Settling on my tried and tested method of tiptoeing up every step, avoiding the parts I've already memorised as squeaky, I make it to Cari's bedroom without disturbing Seren.

I place the wine and glasses on her small dressing table and strip off my shirt, then I lie back against her mound of pillows.

My mind replays the events of today, from my family and their easy acceptance, to Seren's permanent smile. I'm surprised she hasn't flapped her little hands right off.

I close my eyes and remember watching Cari in the pool with her. The small, emerald green swimsuit, setting off her porcelain colouring and highlighting her auburn hair, making her look every inch, my fiery auburn, angel.

I store the images away, locked up tight in the growing memory file that houses my perfect days.

Before, I could count my perfect days on one hand, now I know every day is perfect because I get to spend them with her.

chapter 29

Cari

I stay a little longer in the shower than I intended, I think it's due to daydreaming under the hot spray about how well today went.

How perfect it was.

When I walk into my bedroom, I expect to find Liam naked and sipping wine, instead he's out cold.

His firm, muscled chest rises and falls with his deep breathing and I inch closer needing to drink in more of him.

His face is the picture of serenity, his full lips are relaxed and slightly parted in sleep and his dark eyelashes flutter ever so slightly, betraying the dreams that must play beneath his lids.

He's even more beautiful like this; unguarded, open and to some extent, vulnerable. It makes me want to smother him in his own protective suit of love, one I am the tailor of.

He spends so much time giving his all to

everyone else that I want to give my all to him.

I don't bother to dry off, instead I carefully climb into the bed, still damp from the shower, snuggle into his chest and pull the comforter over us.

When I look back up to his face, his eyes are open and looking right at me. He reaches over and runs his palm over my hip, his eyes flaring in surprise when he registers my nakedness.

"Is it my birthday?"

I blink up at him, "What?"

"Well, you're wet and naked in my bed when I've just opened my eyes from dreaming about you; I'm wondering if I have woken up or if I am, in fact, still dreaming."

I push up on the bed and bring my lips towards his, "Well, you're awake now, let's see if I can make those dreams of yours come true."

He smiles as my mouth hits his, our lips connecting and sending a stream of heat down my spine that ends at the apex of my thighs.

No more is spoken with words; instead we use our lips, our tongues, our hands and fingers to speak of heat, of touch, of lust and of love.

I crawl up his body and lay flush against him, the only barrier between us is his jeans, which I soon make quick work of removing.

Then we are skin to skin, his hardness rubbing over my softness and creating a friction so delicious that I can do nothing but moan.

The need to taste him consumes me and I break

three

our kiss, working my mouth down his body, attempting to kiss every inch of skin along the way.

He shivers every time I find a sensitive spot and it only emboldens me to find more, bringing my tongue into play to tease him, until he's gasping for breath and begging me for more.

"*God, Cari.* I'm about ready to combust; if you don't take me into your sweet, hot mouth soon, I'm going to flip you over and take exactly what I want."

His threat excites me further and I grin around the nipple I'm currently laving with my tongue. I want him to take me, to dominate me and to show me just how much he wants me.

I edge my way across his chest to lick and suckle his other nipple, but before I can get there I am picked up and deposited flat on my back in the middle of the bed.

He kneels over me, the plains of his chest even more defined in the lamplight, his strong thighs just calling to be touched and his impressive length, jutting out begging to be licked.

He runs his eyes greedily over my body and wherever they look, his fingers soon follow; touching, caressing, squeezing, flicking. Driving me as wild as I just drove him.

"*Fuck*, you are beautiful. I wish I could paint you just like this."

Breathing laboured and eyelids heavy, I connect my eyes with his, "Then paint me, but first, *fuck me*. I need you, Liam."

A cheeky grin spreads across his mouth and out pops that single dimple I long to taste with my tongue, "Not so fast, Miss Pritchard. I seem to remember the need to spank you," he watches as my eyes flare wide with hesitation, "Now, now, Cariad, fair's fair. If I can't spank you, I'm going to have to take that pretty mouth of yours and fill it with my cock."

My reply is to open my mouth wide and reach out for his erection; it swells even further at my touch and I'm determined to make him crazy with my mouth and tongue.

I lean up on one elbow and use my hand to guide him into my mouth, quickly darting out my tongue to taste the first drops of his arousal.

His entire body shivers and the power in giving him this, in controlling his pleasure, only seeks to ratchet up my own desire.

I run my tongue over the broad head, flicking it against the sensitive underside and a groan tears out of his throat.

Using my hand to cup his firm balls, I work my mouth down his length, taking as much of him as I can, before sucking hard and dragging my mouth back up. After only a few strokes from my mouth, he's pulling out and flipping me over onto my knees.

I nearly collapse when I feel his mouth lick straight up my pussy, from clit to entrance; a ragged breath escaping my lips at the sensation of his firm, warm and wet tongue doing delicious things to my

three

already over-sensitive private parts.

I grind shamelessly against him, seeking out more, needing to find my release, but he denies me, pulling back to blow warm air over my wet centre and causing me to cry out from the loss of friction.

Before I can protest too much, he's positioned himself at my entrance and drives straight in. His balls smacking against my throbbing clit, almost making me orgasm from just one thrust.

He pulls back out just as quickly and pounds straight back in, building a pace that soon threatens to tip me over the edge.

Then he brings his talented fingers in to play and uses one hand to rub circles around my swollen clit, the other he uses on my nipples; tugging and pinching with firm yet gentle movements.

I am no longer Cari, I am only sensations and electricity and on his next powerful thrust, I come undone; my body feels like it's floating towards the ceiling before it collapses on the bed.

But he's not done, he stills inside me balls deep and rides the wave of my orgasm before he pulling out and gently turning me over.

Then, he continues to make love to me with slow thrusts and feather-light touches, until another wave of bliss rolls through me and a few moments later, he finds his own release.

"Move in with me?"

I blame my question on post-coital rapture.

The two orgasms I've just had, clouding my rational brain in a fog of euphoria.

He stills behind me; we lie spooned, legs tangled, bed sheet pulled up to our waists.

Panicking, I go to move to take back the stupid words I've just spoken, but he pins me to his front, his softening cock twitching against my rear.

"Move in with you?"

His sex thickened voice runs over my skin, leaving goose bumps in its path.

"I…I didn't mean to…what I meant was…"

"Ask me again."

His voice is deep and filled with need.

I hesitate, not wanting to hear the reasons why it wouldn't be a good idea. His hands wrap around me tightly, their strength pledging to never let me go and I find my voice to ask again.

"Move in with me, with us?"

His arms tighten further and I wonder if I can keep breathing if he doesn't ease up soon.

"I would like that more than anything, to be able to come home to you both every day but I need you to be sure Cari, don't ask me if you have any doubts."

This time, when I try to move, he eases his hold and I wiggle myself around in his arms so I can face him.

"When I heard Jake ask you today about whether

three

you had found a place, my heart dropped. I don't know why, it's silly really, but I always thought that if you ever left your parents, it would be to come and live here with us."

I lift my downcast eyes to his face; his brow is furrowed and I gently use my index finger to trace the lines and soothe them away.

"I understand if it's too big of a commitment to ask of you right now. I mean, we've only been together again for a few weeks..."

"Stop," he stills my hand and draws my gaze back to his face, "You're talking to me, no one else is here, it's just us, so you don't need to worry about what words to use or if you've said the right thing." He takes my hand and places it on his chest, directly above his heart.

"I never thought, not for one second, you were ready for this step and more than that, I never assumed it would be okay to force myself into your life and into Seren's, but now you've said it, now you've planted the seed in my head, it's taken root and grown into something I know I want more than anything."

He leans forward and gently kisses my forehead, continuing to whisper softly over my skin, "I'd love to move in here with you; to have more and more perfect days and to be here for you when those days happen to be less than perfect."

I close my eyes and absorb his words, "I guess it's settled then, whenever you're ready to move out of your parent's place, you can come home here, to us."

"Tomorrow."

I open my eyes and chuckle, "Tomorrow you will be busy enough with the presentation day and both Seren and I will be there to see you do something amazing. I'm not sure you can fit in a house move too."

"You're right, the following day it is then."

I sigh and lay my head against his chest, the strong thump of his heart echoing through my blood and finding its beat deep inside my own.

"The following day sounds perfect."

chapter 30

Liam

All the arrangements have been made; Cari and Seren are already there, my parents have just left along with the rest of the Fox-Williams clan so that just leaves me and Jules.

She arrives to pick me up in a chauffeur driven Bentley, Jake insisting she needed protection.

She rolled her eyes at his overprotectiveness, but I guess being thousands of miles away, he just wanted to make sure his wife would be safe.

I don't blame him, even if we are only going to a small special needs school, it's better to be safe than sorry and he has picked up more than his fair share of crazy fans.

"Hey, Li. You all set?" Jules has rolled down her window and is calling over to me from the back seat of her ride.

"Yeah, all ready. I just gotta go and grab the ridiculously huge cheque you made me order from the bank. Seriously, who does that anymore?"

She laughs at me and shakes her head, "Everyone who wants to gain press attention when giving away a large amount of money does it."

I grab the metre long, cardboard cheque and walk towards the car, "But I don't want press attention and as far as I am aware, neither do you."

"It's not about us, it's about the school and the foundation. This exposure could bring us more big money backers and get the school even more donations."

I try and fail to force the humongous check into the boot of the car, so I open the passenger door and force it into the back with me and Jules.

"You were saying, exposure…blah, blah, blah…more money…blah, blah blah…giant cheque rammed in your face for an entire journey. That's about all I heard."

She forces the cheque towards the floor, then bats me on the arm, "You're such a moany, big baby today."

"Am not."

"Are too. So what's got your knickers in a twist?"

"My knickers aren't in a twist. Will you stop pestering me and just give the nod to Big Guy One and Big Guy Two in the front that we're ready to

three

go."

She stares at me for a long moment and then tells her driver we are ready to depart.

"Now we are on the move, can you untwist your knickers because I think they are stopping the blood from getting to your nuts and, therefore, are cutting off the air supply to your brain."

She chuckles after trying and failing to deliver her reply in a cutting fashion, "Oh for heaven's sake, just talk to me, Li. That's what friends are for."

I scowl at her and then decide I need to spill it or else my mood is just going to get worse.

"Mum knows about me and Cari."

Her eyebrows scrunch together in that cute way they always do when she doesn't understand something, "Well, duh, of course she does, you're bloody moving in with her tomorrow."

"No, you're not getting me, *she knows.*" I surreptitiously glance at her bodyguards, uncomfortable about airing my dirty laundry to an audience.

"Hey," she calls my attention back to her, "Bob and Shaun have both signed non-disclosure agreements, pretend they aren't even here and talk to me. Now, I'm still confused so you're gonna have to spell it out for me."

I huff out an annoyed breath, my voice getting louder in the process until I'm all but shouting, "She *knows* I was barely eighteen when I first slept with Cari, she *knows* we had an affair while she was still my teacher. She. Knows. Everything."

Jules looks at me in utter disbelief, "I never said a word to anyone, I swear."

I scrub my hand down my face, trying to calm myself, "I know you didn't, I never thought for one second that you did. When she confronted me this morning, I asked her what on earth made her concoct such a story, even though the denial felt like acid on my tongue. She told me, 'A mother just knows; I've always known, from the very start,' so you see, I'm sat here with you now, unable to let Cari know my mother is aware of our deepest, darkest, secret and the one she has begged me to never tell. I can't warn her for fear of her doing a runner and I'm totally helpless to stop Mum from confronting Cari any minute now."

I stare at Jules, hoping for some wise words of advice, instead I get, "*Holy fucking shit.*"

"Holy fucking shit indeed, now can you see why my knickers are more than twisted, they are positively choking me."

For once, Jules is totally out of advice, well, that's a lie, she finally says, "Just take it as it comes. I don't think Honor would confront her at the school, so I'll intercept Cari when I can and try and to keep them apart until you can speak to your mother again."

I slump back in my seat, throwing up a silent prayer to the universe that today doesn't go completely tits up.

three

"We are overwhelmed by the generous donation of fifty thousand pounds from the Fox Foundation; it will not only complete our rebound therapy room and new art studio but will also buy all the equipment necessary to keep us in supplies for both of these rooms for the next few years."

A loud round of applause ripples across the yard and I scan my eyes over all the faces in front of me, immediately finding Cari in the front row.

She is wearing a face-splitting grin and clapping more vigorously than anyone else around her. I can't help but smile back at the pride that pours off her for me.

I let my eyes scan the crowd further and spot my entire family, minus Jake who's winging his way to Canada for filming and my gaze lands on my mother. She's not looking at the small stage area like everyone else, she's looking directly at Cari and I can't tell if the look on her face is a small smile or a grimace.

Fuck. My. Life.

"And now, I'd like to welcome to the stage the couple that made all this happen, Emma Fox and Liam Fox-Williams. Both are here today to represent the Fox Foundation and without whom, we wouldn't be celebrating today. A round of applause for our guests of honour, ladies and gentlemen if you please."

The clapping is even louder than before; my family even throws in a few whoops and whistles.

Jules takes the mic and soon has the large crowd

entranced with her passionate speech about the foundation and all that it stands for.

A small group of photographers click away, almost blinding me with their flashes and make it harder to track the crowd. My eyes still flick between two of the most important women in my life; women that may be about to come to blows.

Jules introduces me, but I am so consumed with staring at my Mum and Cari, I totally miss my cue.

"Now I would like to invite Liam to talk to you about his involvement with this project...Liam?"

I am oblivious to all the eyes now on me and continue to stare out into the crowd.

She clears her voice and gives a light chuckle, "I think he might have a little stage fright," the crowd laughs, "Liam," she nudges me with her elbow shaking me from my trance, "Do you have a few words to say?"

I can feel colour filling my cheeks but mentally shake it off to deliver the words I've already memorised, words Cari helped me to write.

"I...ah...I think the magnitude of the day has finally gotten to me. I'm not normally this tongue tied, I promise," a small ripple of laughter passes through the crowd.

I lock eyes with Cari and she gives me a double thumbs up, the stupid grin on her face, combined with her overenthusiastic hand signal, makes me smile.

"I paid a visit to Trinity Waters a few weeks ago

three

and I'll let you in on a secret, my reasons for coming weren't completely selfless," I am completely ignoring my script and instead begin speaking from my heart.

"You see, I've met this amazing woman, a woman who has had more pain and loss in her life than any one person should have to endure."

I look directly at Cari, whose hand is pressed against her chest, tears already threatening to spill over and I have to move my gaze before I lose my resolve.

"This amazing woman is not amazing because she's survived; she's not amazing because she has her scars, she's not even amazing because she got through a terrible time in her life and came out a better and stronger person. She's amazing because she did all that and still managed to put someone else and their needs before herself."

I catch my mother's eye and see hers filled with tears, my father stepping in to wrap his arm around her and pull her close.

"I fell in love with this amazing woman, even when she didn't want me to," again, I look to Cari.

I chuckle to myself, "So what's a guy to do when the woman of his dreams won't even give him a chance?" The crowd laughs with me.

"I found out who she sacrificed a large part of her life for, in the hopes of understanding. Only the knowledge I gained only served to make me have even more questions and I found myself banging on

Mr. Thomas' door," I look towards the Head Master and he smiles at me to continue.

"You see, this amazing woman cares...no that's not a strong enough word...she *adores*, she *worships* and she *loves*, an equally amazing little girl. A little girl who sees wonder in the things we may think are ordinary, who finds joy in simple activities such as watching the leaves blow on the trees or the waves on a shore, a little girl who struggles with what we consider average day-to-day life, every, single, day."

I look down to my hands, my thoughts filled with Seren.

"This little girl has severe Autism and for me that word was so foreign, so abstract, I didn't even know where to start. I trawled the internet, yet only got more confused and so I set up a meeting with Mr. Thomas, hoping to pick his brains."

I look back around the crowd to find everyone hanging on my words, "What started out as a fact-finding visit, soon evolved into something bigger, something *more*. My eyes were opened up by this inspirational school that is filled with extraordinary students and all their wonderful teachers and in opening my eyes, it also opened up my soul. That visit changed me as a person and I will be forever thankful to Mr. Thomas and Trinity Waters."

If I thought the crowd was loud before, it's nothing compared to the cheers that fill the air when I've finished speaking.

When the applause finally dies down, a lone

three

voice calls out from the assembled press, "So, what we want to know is, did you get the girl in the end? Did the woman you refer to as amazing give you a chance?"

I stare straight at Cari and I'm aware most of the crowd has followed my gaze.

"She gave me something far more valuable than just a chance, she gave me her heart."

With the presentation over, most people mill around outside chatting and enjoying the refreshments that are provided.

The inside of the school is out of bounds for such a large crowd as Mr. Thomas explained to everyone that summer school is still taking place today and he was not prepared to disrupt the children's routines.

I am already aware of this because Cari dropped Seren here this morning, long before everyone else arrived for the event.

From the moment both Jules and I stepped down from the stage, we have been engulfed with questions from the press and well wishes from the attendees.

I smile politely and shake many hands when all I really want to do is get back to Cari.

A hand clasps my shoulder and I turn to find Isaac smiling broadly, "Epic speech, Li-Li."

My attempt at returning his smile must look

forced and my eyes flick behind him searching out anyone else from my family, hopefully, my mother or Cari.

"If you're looking for your girl, she's with Mum and Dad. It's all good, I think they are helping run interference as a few of the paps were trying to get her picture."

Panic overtakes me and I spin around wildly trying to find them in the crowd.

"Chill out, Li-Li, she's safe, the Head Master bloke has taken them inside to see Seren."

"*Fuck.*" My loud curse gains more unwanted attention, "Tell Jules where I'm heading."

I don't have time to explain things further, instead I push my way through the throng, not bothering with polite greetings for the many people who attempt to get in my way.

I enter the school and I'm faced with the same security protocols as before; the older lady who finally gives me a visitor's badge doesn't stop smiling at me.

"That was some speech, young man. She's a lucky girl."

"Umm…thanks. Can you find out where she went and if my parents are with her?"

She continues to smile and buzzes me through the doors, "Oh, that's easy. They all went into the

three

sensory room to see Seren. Do you need me to show you where it is?"

Hurrying through the doors, I absorb her words and almost forget to reply in the rush to get to Cari, "No, no, that's fine. I remember where it is."

Striding through the corridors, I approach the room moments later and hesitate outside. Huffing out a long breath, I run my hand through my hair and turn the handle quietly, reminding myself that Seren is inside and there's no way either woman is going to cause a scene and upset her.

I quietly enter the dark room, to find the only light once again coming from the bubble tube.

Unlike the last time I was here, Seren isn't sat with her carer, instead I find her laying on the padded plinth that houses the bubble tube, my mother laying by her side.

Both are calmly watching the bubbles while it slowly changes colour, first bathing them in a soft red glow, then green, then blue.

A hand softly grips mine and I look to my side right into Cari's beautiful, smiling face.

"Hey," she whispers, leaning herself into my side.

"Hey, right back." I let go of her hand to wrap my arm across her shoulders and hug her to me, her very presence soothing some of my worries.

"That was some speech you gave out there."

I look down at her shadowed form to see her staring up at me, "Yeah, well, I had some good inspiration."

Her arms squeeze tightly around me and my heart rate slows knowing that no confrontation could have happened for her to be so calm.

I glance back over to the bubble tube and see Seren still mesmerized, but my mother's eyes are fixed firmly on me.

She pushes up slowly from her prone position, careful not to disturb Seren and makes her way towards us.

Her hand reaches out to cup my cheek and tears fill her eyes, "I'm so proud to call you my son." I absorb her touch for a moment and then pull away so I can look at her, "Do you have a moment to talk to your favourite son?"

She smiles softly at me, "There's nothing to say right now, my sweet, thoughtful boy," she looks towards Cari and then leans in to embrace her.

"Look after my boy." I hear her whisper into Cari's hair.

They pull back and look at each other, in the soft light from the bubble tube it's hard to tell if either is crying.

Cari leans up to kiss my mother on her cheek, "When a man treats a woman like your son treats me, like a princess he worships and adores, you know it's because he was raised by a queen. Thank you for giving me such an amazing man to love. I promise to protect him with all that I am."

"I know you will. I've always known you two

three

would find each other again." She leans in for one last hug and then turns to me.

"I'm so proud of you, son of mine. You've always been an old soul, always put others before yourself. I worried your generous spirit would make you vulnerable, that the wrong person would take advantage of it," she looks to Cari and then back to me, "Now I realise that like will always find like and the soul will always find its other half."

She takes my face in her hands and places three kisses on it, one on my forehead and one on each cheek, "The past is the past for a reason, do you remember me saying that?"

I nod, while her fingers softly stroke my cheeks, "Then let's leave it where it belongs and look forward to a glorious future."

A few hours later, after dropping Cari and Seren back home, I head back to my parent's house to spend my last night there.

I fully expect a house full when I open the front door, but I am met with silence.

I walk through the rooms, seeing each one empty and hear a noise coming from my Dad's study.

I knock once, open the door and see the familiar scene of my father pouring over numerous, geographical maps.

"Ah, Liam. Come in son. Let me put some of

this away."

He goes about folding the maps and stacking them in a pile on his large oak sideboard, stopping to pour us both a snifter of whisky.

He hands me the crystal tumbler containing two fingers of amber liquid and walks around his desk to sit in his large, leather chair.

"Your mother has gone to tell the WI group that she's pulling out of the cookbook project," he looks over at me from the rim of his glass, "If you ask me, I think she couldn't bear to see her youngest packing up all his stuff." He smiles and sinks back into his chair.

I take a healthy sip of my own drink and relish in the feeling of the heat that flows down my throat and settles in my belly.

"I…did she…what I mean is…"

"Did she discuss the Cariad situation with me?"

I nod once, unable to voice my query.

"We've been married over thirty years, son; there is nothing your mother keeps from me or I from her."

I nod once more and look down into my glass, swirling my drink around and almost causing it to spill over the sides.

"We're not upset with you, son, things…happen and the heart wants what the heart wants. You may have been younger then, but you were in no way a child, in fact, you've always been more grown up than all of your brothers."

three

I look up at my father, the man Jake resembles so much and I notice for the first time, we share the same dimple, in the same spot, that only appears when we grin. The dimple Cari loves so much.

"So, she's not upset with me, not mad with me for keeping it from you both?"

He takes another sip of his drink and replies, "Not mad with you, I don't think your mother is capable of getting mad with any of you. Disappointed you didn't confide in her? Maybe. Sad that you hid your heartache away? Definitely. Upset about you and Cari? Not in the slightest. I think she too has fallen in love with that girl, with both of your girls. She's happy you've found each other again."

I stare out of the window at the darkening sky, "She's it for me, Dad."

"We know, son. We know."

epilogue

Liam

Three years later...

"Time to go, Seren. Say goodbye to Caleb and Aunt Emmy."

Seren puts her hand to her mouth and motions blowing a kiss by patting her lips a few times.

I look over to Jules and my chubby nephew, Caleb, who looks like a mini version of his dad.

Caleb waves with a small flap of his hand and goes back to playing with his toys, "Say hi to the superstar for me when he gets back."

Jules laughs, "He loves it when you call him that, you know. You'd be better off not stroking his ego and just calling him Jake."

"Ah, where's the fun in that. See you next week Jules, bye Caleb."

We walk around the side of the house and head

three

towards the car.

Sunday afternoons at Jules and Jake's place have become a regular occurrence. Cari and Jules are firm friends and you can barely get a word in edgeways when they are together and Seren loves being here. In fact, I think it's her favourite place to visit.

When we put a picture of their house on her schedule, she tries to rush through all the other activities that come before it, in order to try and get here sooner.

This is the first week that Cari hasn't come with us, then again, she needs her sleep so I offered to just take Seren to give her a break.

I just hope Carys, our six-day-old baby girl, has let her mummy rest.

I wanted to bring her too, but Cari didn't want to be without her, so it's just me and my big girl, spending some quality time together with her Aunt and her little cousin.

I'm strapping Seren into the car when Jules' voice comes from behind me, "Cari just called, she said to get some more nappies on your way home."

I shut the door, once I know Seren is settled and turn to face her. Caleb is on her hip and she has her phone in her opposite hand.

"Will do, I think my girl could win awards for the number of nappies she dirties. Can you call her back and tell her I'll grab some at the supermarket on the way back?" I make my way to the driver's side, "Oh, and tell her I'll bring dinner home too. Seren and I are fancying some pizza."

"You mean you are fancying pizza?"

I look towards my brother's wife who is still my best friend, "No, I mean we are. Just because you didn't see her ask, doesn't mean I don't know exactly what my girl needs."

She laughs and shakes her head, walking backwards towards the house, "Yeah, yeah. You sound just like Jake when he tells me Caleb made him open an extra beer."

"Beeeeer." Caleb butts in, making us both laugh.

"See you in the week Jules…oh and don't forget…"

"Oh, for heaven's sake, how am I going to forget that I'm helping you shop next week. It's only once a lifetime that a girl gets to help chose a ring for her best friend, to propose to another of her best friends."

She turns and begins to walk away, "I'll pick you up Wednesday at 9 am sharp."

She lifts her hand and gives me a limp wave of dismissal, Caleb copying her action with a big smile on his chubby cheeks.

After a quick pit stop at the supermarket for nappies

three

and a call to the pizza place to arrange a delivery, Seren and I get back home to a very quiet house.

Hoping Cari has managed to get back to sleep, I guide Seren into the living room and find Cari fast asleep on the sofa, with a sleepy Carys on her chest.

Mindful of not making too much noise and waking them both, I quickly grab Seren's iPad and pop on her headphones, settling her in her favourite armchair with a drink and a biscuit to buy me some more quiet time.

I look around at the three most important people in my life and laugh silently to myself; I am totally outnumbered by females.

My eyes land on Seren, then Cari and finally on our newest addition; Carys is the image of her mother, with a tuft of auburn hair and baby soft porcelain skin. She is the missing piece of our puzzle, a surprise gift that although unplanned, is very much wanted.

As I stand, surrounded by my girls, I have the urge to capture this scene on canvas.

We are no longer *three*, we are *four*.

Four suits in a pack of cards, yet these girls will always be my hearts.

Four seasons; my spring, my summer, my autumn and my winter.

Four points of a compass, guiding me home.

special dedication

This book is, quite simply, about love.

Love comes in many forms; one of the purest is the love between a parent and their child.

All the best parents sacrifice things for their children, but the sacrifices that I see made by parents of children with special needs, is, without a doubt, the most powerful love I have ever seen.

Love is measured by the decisions we take every day; it's often tested during the dark and challenging moments and it shines brightest when a person puts their life second, to ensure another not just copes, but thrives.

So, this book is for all the warrior mothers, fathers, brothers, sisters and grandparents who sacrifice daily, to ensure their children live life to the fullest.

It is also for my warrior husband and warrior son; I would be lost without you both.

Last, but not least, it is for my two, special, spectrum princesses.

Who needs black and white when we have all the colours of the rainbow?

playlist

Scars – James Bay
Hourglass – Catfish and the Bottlemen
Cocoon – Catfish and the Bottlemen
Do I Wanna Know – Arctic Monkeys
Lightening Bolt – Jake Bugg
Hedonism – Skunk Anasie
Seven Years – Norah Jones
Make You Feel My Love – Adele
Opposite – Biffy Clyro
Tonight, Tonight – The Smashing Pumpkins
I Miss You – Blink 182
Good Riddance (Time of My Life) – Green Day
The Blower's Daughter – Damien Rice
How Long Will I Love You – Ellie Goulding
You've Got The Love – Candi Staton

acknowledgments

I am blessed to have met so many amazing people since I hit publish on my first book.

To all the authors who have supported me on my writing journey, including the amazing SITL group; you ladies ROCK!

Special, BIG snogs to my 'Southern Hemisphere Twin', the lovely KA Sterritt, who keeps me sane, listens to my crazy ramblings and always has my back.

To the crazy ladies in my reader's group 'E's Elite'. All the best people are bonkers and you lot definitely are. Thank you for your support, your friendships and your random posts that often require me to pull out my bottle of eye bleach. (Don't you dare say it's my fault or I'll cook the goat, banish the nuns and drown the mermaids!)

HUGE thanks to my Ah-mazing beta readers. Cynthia, Mary, Sharon, Nicola, Alexandra and Rebecca, your support is unending and this book would not look the way it does without you.

To all the blogs who took a chance on a new indie author, and not only read and reviewed, but recommended, pimped, promoted me and for no other reason than they love to do so. BIG SNOGS for you always.

Finally, for you, the readers. I wouldn't be here without you. Thank you for your passion, your reviews and your support of authors, be they traditional or indie.

Bookworms will rule the world!

about the author

Eli Carter is a mum of three from the U.K.

She is a stay-at-home mum and a part-time advocate for families of children with special needs.

Her life is pretty manic and she often gets asked, "How do you find the time to write?"

The answer is simple, she never sleeps, but not from lack of trying.

Reading and writing is her therapy, her solace and often the one thing that get's her through the long nights. (That and copious amounts of caffeine and sugar!)

She loves to connect with readers, so please feel free to friend/follow her on Facebook, follow her on IG and Twitter or join her reader's group, E's Elite.

Facebook: www.facebook.com/escarterauthor
IG: @escarterauthor
Twitter: @escarterauthor

Made in the USA
Charleston, SC
08 March 2016